TERMINATOR 2®
JUDGMENT DAY

THE OFFICIAL GRAPHIC NOVEL ADAPTATION

IBOOKS GRAPHIC NOVELS

Vietnam Journal
by Don Lomax

Vic and Blood:
The Continuing Adventures of a Boy and His Dog
by Harlan Ellison and Richard Corben

Honour Among Punks:
The Complete Baker Street Collection
by Gary Reed and Guy Davis

Raymond Chandler's Marlowe
by Tom DeHaven & Rian Hughes,
Jerome Charyn & David Lloyd,
and James Rose, Lee Moyer & Alfredo Alcala

The Best of Ray Bradbury: The Graphic Novel
by Ray Bradbury, et al.

Yossel: April 19, 1943
by Joe Kubert

Sunn
by Steven A. Roman,
Kevin Lau, and Alex Niño

TERMINATOR 2®
JUDGMENT DAY
THE GRAPHIC NOVEL

ADAPTATION BY
GREGORY WRIGHT

ART BY
KLAUS JANSON

BASED ON THE
SCREENPLAY BY
JAMES CAMERON
AND WILLIAM WISHER

ibooks
new york
www.ibooks.net

DISTRIBUTED BY SIMON & SCHUSTER, INC.

A Publication of ibooks, inc.

Based on the world created in the screenplay
written by James Cameron and William Wisher

Distributed by Simon & Schuster, Inc.
1230 Avenue of the Americas, New York, NY 10020

ibooks, inc.
24 West 25th Street
New York, NY 10010

The ibooks World Wide Web Site Address is:
http://www.ibooks.net

ISBN 0-7434-7992-0
First ibooks, inc. printing October 2003
10 9 8 7 6 5 4 3 2 1

TERMINATOR 2®: JUDGMENT DAY
Edited by Bobbie Chase

TERMINATOR 2®: CYBERNETIC DAWN
Edited by Dan Shaheen

Cover design by Brendan Hitt

Printed in Canada

LOS ANGELES,
JULY 11, 2029
3 BILLION LIVES ENDED ON AUGUST 29TH, 1997. THE SURVIVORS OF THE NUCLEAR FIRE CALLED THE WAR JUDGMENT DAY. THEY LIVED ONLY TO FACE A NEW NIGHTMARE, THE WAR AGAINST THE MACHINES...
SKYNET, THE COMPUTER WHICH CONTROLLED THE MACHINES, SENT TWO TERMINATORS BACK THROUGH TIME. THEIR MISSION: TO DESTROY THE LEADER OF THE HUMAN RESISTANCE...
JOHN CONNOR. MY SON.

ZZZKKT
ZZZKKT
PRESENT DAY.
THE FIRST TERMINATOR WAS PROGRAMMED TO STRIKE AT ME, IN THE YEAR 1984...BEFORE JOHN WAS BORN. IT FAILED.
ZZKKT
KKKRRRKKKK!!
THE SECOND WAS SET TO STRIKE AT JOHN HIMSELF, WHEN HE WAS STILL A CHILD. AS BEFORE, THE RESISTANCE WAS ABLE TO SEND A LONE WARRIOR. A PROTECTOR FOR JOHN.
IT WAS JUST A QUESTION OF WHICH ONE OF THEM WOULD REACH HIM FIRST...
I NEED YOUR CLOTHES, YOUR BOOTS, AND YOUR MOTORCYCLE.
YOU FORGOT TO SAY PLEASE.

KRAK!
YEEOOOW!
UH OH.
KREESH
IT SLICES...
IT DICES...
SSSSSSSSSSSSS
AHHRRRR!
...IT...OH, YOU KEEP IT...
EEE!!!EE!!
SHUNK
Y-YOU AIN'T GETTING NUTHIN' FROM ME...
OH, MAN... OH, MAN...
UH...ON SECOND THOUGHT...M-MAYBE WE CAN MAKE A DEAL?

ELSEWHERE...
KKKKKKRRRRKK
WHAT IN THE...
SSKREEEEEEEEEEEE
BIZARRE...
WHO...?
WAK

"THE NEXT PATIENT IS A 29-YEAR-OLD FEMALE DIAGNOSED AS SUFFERING FROM ACUTE SCHIZO-AFFECTIVE DISORDER.
"THE USUAL INDICATORS... DEPRESSION, ANXIETY, VIOLENT ACTING OUT, DELUSIONS OF PERSECUTION. WE KEEP HER IN MAXIMUM SECURITY."

...23...24... 25...
MORNING, SARAH.
GOOD MORNING, DR. SILBERMAN. HOW'S THE KNEE?
SHE UH... STABBED ME IN THE KNEE-CAP WITH MY PEN A FEW WEEKS AGO. THE DELUSIONAL ARCHITECTURE IS INTERESTING.
SHE BELIEVES A MACHINE CALLED A TERMINATOR, WHICH LOOKS HUMAN OF COURSE, WAS SENT THROUGH TIME TO KILL HER.
AND ALSO THAT THE FATHER OF HER CHILD WAS A SOLDIER, SENT TO PROTECT HER... HE WAS FROM THE FUTURE, TOO...
HA!
THE YEAR 2029, IF I REMEMBER CORRECTLY. LET'S MOVE ON, SHALL WE?
DOUGLAS, I DON'T LIKE THE PATIENTS DISRUPTING THEIR ROOMS LIKE THIS. SEE THAT SHE TAKES HER THORAZINE, WOULD YOU?
BIG FUN.

TIME TO TAKE YOUR MEDS, CONNOR.
YOU TAKE IT.
NOW YOU KNOW YOU GOT TO BE GOOD 'CAUSE YOU'RE UP FOR REVIEW THIS AFTERNOON...
I'M NOT TAKING IT. NOW I DON'T WANT ANY TROUBLE...

AIN'T NO TROUBLE AT ALL--
YOU SON OF A-- WHOOF!

LAST CALL, SUGAR.

YOUR FOSTER PARENTS ARE KINDA DORKS, HUH, JOHN?

JOHN? I'M TALK--WHOA! HEY MAN, EASY ON THE TURNS...
DERAL SECURITY BANK
RRRRRRRMMMM

EASY MONEY.
YOU SURE THIS'LL WORK?
NO PROBLEMO.

WHERE'D YOU LEARN ALL THIS STUFF?

FROM MY MOM. MY REAL MOM, I MEAN.
EXCELLENT! GOT IT! LET'S GO!

LATER.
THAT YOUR REAL MOM?
YEAH, THAT'S HER.
SO SHE'S PRETTY COOL, HUH?
ACTUALLY, NO, SHE'S A COMPLETE PSYCHO. THAT'S WHY SHE'S UP AT PESCADERO. SHE TRIED TO BLOW UP A COMPUTER FACTORY, BUT GOT SHOT AND ARRESTED.

Juvenile Division
Subject: Connor, John
Theft, burglary, vandalis
Mother: Connor, Sarah
Legal Guardians: Voigh
Todd & Janelle
523 S. Almond St.,
Reseda, CA

ARE YOU THE LEGAL GUARDIAN OF JOHN CONNOR?
THAT'S RIGHT, OFFICER. WHAT'S HE DONE *NOW*?
COULD I SPEAK WITH HIM, PLEASE?
HE TOOK OFF ON HIS BIKE THIS MORNING... COULD BE *ANY*WHERE.
YOU GONNA TELL ME WHAT THIS IS ABOUT?
I JUST NEED TO ASK HIM A FEW QUESTIONS.
THERE WAS A BIG GUY ON A MOTORCYCLE HERE THIS MORNING ASKING ABOUT HIM, TOO. HAS THAT GOT SOMETHING TO DO WITH IT?

I WOULDN'T WORRY.
"DO YOU HAVE A PHOTOGRAPH OF JOHN?"
LET'S CHECK OUT THE MALL, JOHN!
"UH--YES. GET THE ALBUM, JANELLE."

IT'S NOT JUST A DREAM, YOU MORON!
I'M SURE IT FEELS VERY REAL TO YOU--
ON AUGUST 29, 1997 IT'S GOING TO FEEL PRETTY FREAKING REAL TO YOU TOO! ANYBODY NOT WEARING NUMBER TWO MILLION SUNBLOCK IS GOING TO HAVE A REAL BAD DAY!
I WAS AFRAID... CONFUSED. I FEEL BETTER, NOW. CLEARER.
CLIK

YES. YOUR ATTITUDE HAS BEEN VERY POSITIVE LATELY.
IT HAS HELPED ME TO HAVE A GOAL.
AND WHAT IS THAT?

YOU SAID I COULD BE TRANSFERRED TO A MINIMUM SECURITY WING AND HAVE VISITORS IF I SHOWED IMPROVEMENT IN SIX MONTHS.
WELL, IT'S BEEN SIX MONTHS, AND I WAS LOOKING FORWARD TO SEEING MY SON.
I SEE. LET'S GO BACK TO WHAT YOU WERE SAYING ABOUT THESE TERMINATOR MACHINES.

NOW YOU THINK THEY DON'T EXIST?
THEY DON'T EXIST. I SEE THAT NOW.

BUT YOU'VE TOLD ME ON MANY OCCASIONS ABOUT HOW YOU CRUSHED ONE IN A HYDRAULIC PRESS!
IF I HAD, THERE WOULD HAVE BEEN SOME EVIDENCE. THEY WOULD HAVE FOUND SOMETHING IN THE FACTORY.

I SEE. SO YOU DON'T BELIEVE ANYMORE THAT THE COMPANY COVERED IT UP?
NO. I DON'T.

Cyerdyne Systems

GREETINGS, TROOPS.
MR. DYSON? THE MATERIALS TEAM WANTS TO RUN ANOTHER TEST ON THE UH... ON *IT.*
YUP. C'MON, I'LL GET IT.

LISTEN, MR. DYSON, I KNOW I HAVEN'T BEEN HERE THAT LONG, BUT I WAS WONDERING IF YOU COULD TELL ME... I MEAN, IF YOU KNOW...
KNOW WHAT?

WELL... WHERE *IT* CAME FROM.

I ASKED THEM THAT QUESTION ONCE. KNOW WHAT THEY TOLD ME?

DON'T ASK.
BUT I STILL WONDER...

SO WHAT DO YOU THINK, DOCTOR? I'VE SHOWN A LOT OF IMPROVEMENT, HAVEN'T I?
YOU SEE, SARAH... HERE'S THE PROBLEM. I KNOW HOW SMART YOU ARE, AND I THINK YOU'RE JUST TELLING ME WHAT I WANT TO HEAR.

I DON'T THINK YOU REALLY BELIEVE WHAT YOU'VE BEEN TELLING ME.
PLEASE... MY SON'S IN DANGER... LET ME CALL--
I'M AFRAID NOT. I'M RECOMMENDING THAT YOU STAY HERE ANOTHER SIX MONTHS.

NO!
ARRRH! LET ME GO! SILBERMAN! YOU DON'T KNOW WHAT YOU'RE DOING! YOU IDIOT! YOU'RE DEAD! YOU HEAR ME?!
MODEL CITIZEN!

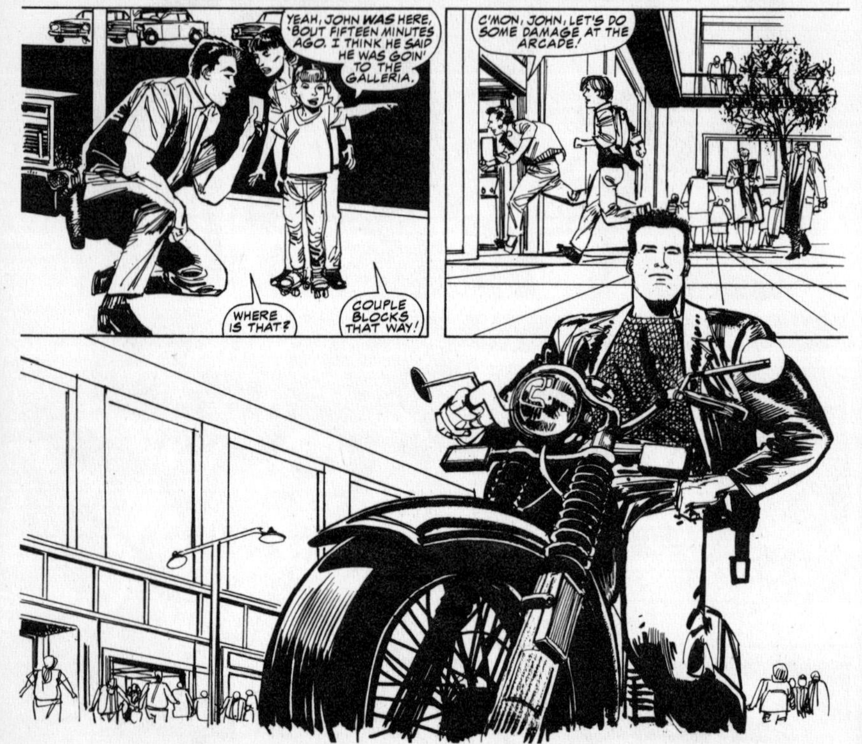
YEAH, JOHN WAS HERE, 'BOUT FIFTEEN MINUTES AGO. I THINK HE SAID HE WAS GOIN' TO THE GALLERIA.
WHERE IS THAT?
COUPLE BLOCKS THAT WAY!
C'MON, JOHN, LET'S DO SOME DAMAGE AT THE ARCADE!

SOME COP IS SCOPING FOR YOU, DUDE.
THIS IS BOGUS, MAN! LATER!
HEY!
OW!
OUGHTTA BE ABLE TO LOSE THE PIG--
HOLY--WHO IN THE--
SHKK CHAKK
GAME OVER, MAN! I'M SCREWED!
GET DOWN.
OMIGOD. OMIGOD.
K-CHOW K-CHOW K-CHOW K-CHOW

YOUHEAND-
LIKEWOWMAN-
HEYHELOOKS...
HE'S ALIVE?
BLAM
BLAM
BLAM
KLIK
KLIK
BLAM
BLAM
BLAM
BLAM
BLAM
BLAM
KLIK
KLIK
MOVE IT, JOHN!
EXIT
GEEZ, WOULDJA LOOKIT DAT!

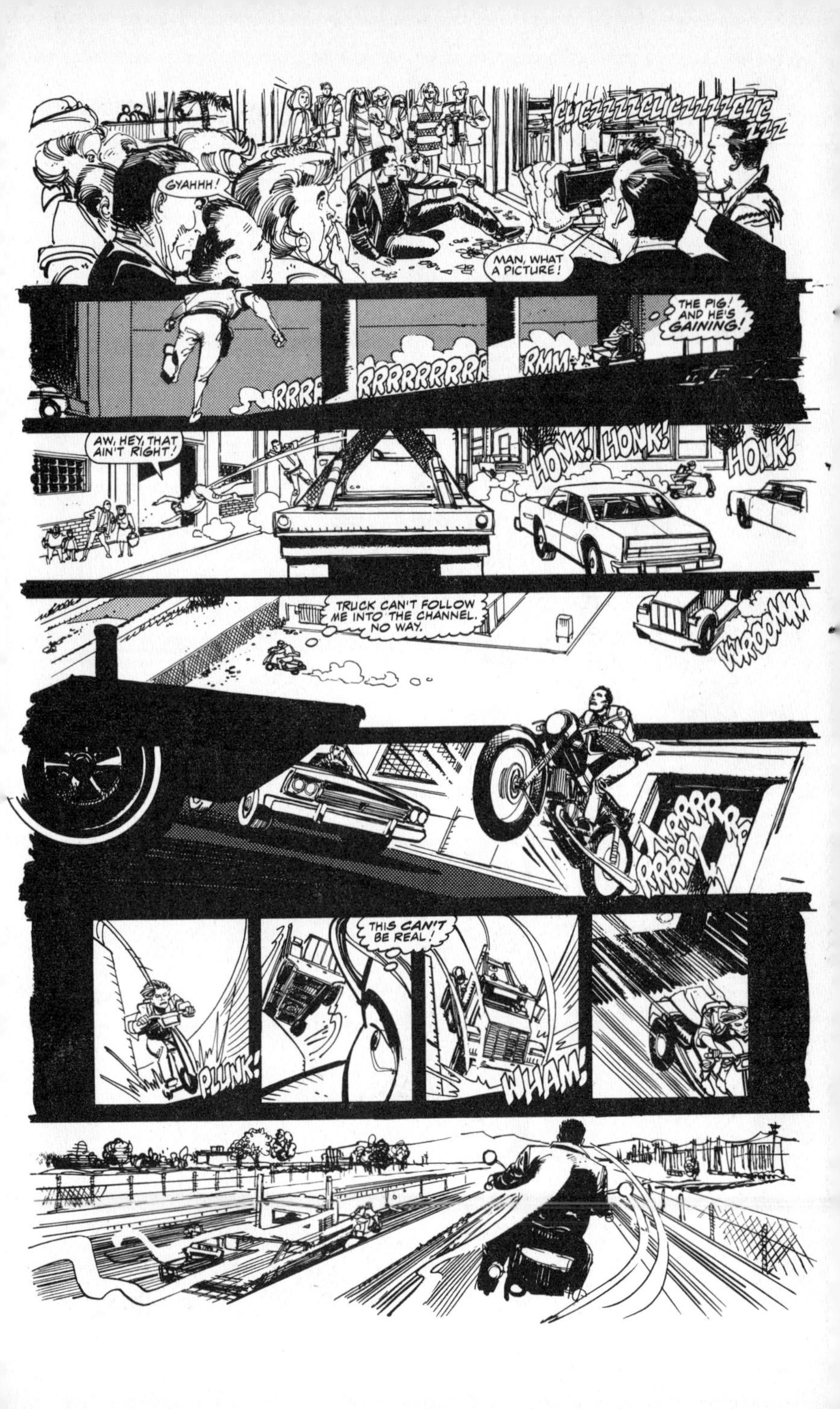

GYAHHH!
MAN, WHAT A PICTURE!
THE PIG! AND HE'S GAINING!
RRRR RRRRRRRRRR RMM
AW, HEY, THAT AIN'T RIGHT!
HONK! HONK!
HONK!
TRUCK CAN'T FOLLOW ME INTO THE CHANNEL. NO WAY.
VVROOMM
THIS CAN'T BE REAL!
PLUNK!
WHAM!

KRAK
I'M NOT BUYIN' IT FOR YOU, PAL!
RRRRRRRRRRM
KRAK!
WHOAH!
BRUNCH
WHOOOOSSHHH
CHOOM!

SHORTLY...
NOW DON'T TAKE THIS THE WRONG WAY, BUT YOU *ARE* A *TERMINATOR*... RIGHT?
YES. CYBERDYNE SYSTEMS, MODEL 101.
HOLY-- Y-YOU'RE REALLY *REAL!* I MEAN ...WHOAH!
MOM *WAS* RIGHT...
YOU'RE, UH... LIKE A MACHINE UNDERNEATH--
I'M A CYBERNETIC ORGANISM. LIVING TISSUE OVER A METAL ENDOSKELETON.
YOU'RE *NOT* HERE TO KILL ME...

MY MISSION IS TO PROTECT YOU.
WHO SENT YOU?

YOU DID.
THIRTY-FIVE YEARS FROM NOW YOU REPROGRAMMED ME TO BE YOUR PROTECTOR HERE, IN THIS TIME.

THIS IS *DEEP*.

SO THIS OTHER GUY? HE'S A TERMINATOR LIKE YOU?
NOT LIKE ME. A T-1000. ADVANCED PROTOTYPE. A MIMETIC POLYALLOY. LIQUID METAL.

RADICAL.
YOU ARE TARGETED FOR TERMINATION. THE T-1000 WILL NOT STOP UNTIL IT COMPLETES ITS MISSION. EVER.

CAN WE STOP BY MY HOUSE?
NEGATIVE. THE T-1000 WILL DEFINITELY TRY TO REACQUIRE YOU THERE.

YOU *SURE?*
I WOULD.
TODD AND JANELLE *ARE* DORKS, BUT I GOTTA *WARN* THEM!
TELEPHONE

JANELLE? IT'S JOHN.
HONEY? WHERE ARE YOU?
SOMETHING'S WRONG. SHE'S NEVER THIS NICE.
WOOFWOOF-WOOFWOOF

MAX'S REALLY BARKING, TOO...
JOHN? SWEETHEART?
I'M HERE. WHAT'S WOLFY BARKING AT?
TELEPHONE

THAT'S MY VOICE!
WOLFY'S JUST EXCITED.
YOUR FOSTER PARENTS ARE DEAD. LET'S GO.

PESCADERO STATE
1416 W KNOLL
Los ANGLES

YOU'RE TELLING ME IT CAN IMITATE ANYTHING IT TOUCHES?!
ONLY OBJECTS OF EQUAL SIZE. NOT COMPLEX MACHINES.
THIS ISN'T THRILLING NEWS.

MOM TOLD ME STUFF LIKE THIS. THAT'S WHY SHE DID WHAT SHE DID. SHE'D SHACK UP WITH ANYONE SHE COULD LEARN MILITARY JUNK FROM...

...SO SHE COULD TEACH ME TO BE THIS GREAT MILITARY LEADER. THEN SHE GETS BUSTED AND IT'S LIKE, SORRY, KID, YOUR MOM'S A PSYCHO!
LIKE, EVERYTHING I WAS BROUGHT UP ON WAS A FANTASY, RIGHT. I HATED HER FOR THAT.

BUT EVERYTHING SHE SAID WAS TRUE!
WE GOTTA GET HER OUT OF THERE!
NEGATIVE. THE T-1000'S HIGHEST PROBABILITY FOR SUCCESS WOULD BE TO COPY SARAH CONNOR AND WAIT FOR YOU TO MAKE CONTACT.
OH, GREAT. AND WHAT HAPPENS TO HER?
TYPICALLY THE SUBJECT BEING COPIED IS TERMINATED.
TERMINATED?! CRIPES! WHY DIDN'T YOU TELL ME? WE'RE GOIN', NOW!
NEGATIVE. SHE IS NOT A MISSION PRIORITY.

YEAH, WELL KISS MINE. SHE'S A PRIORITY TO ME!
HEY, WHAT'S YOUR PROB? LET ME GO!

YOU HAVE TO DO WHAT I SAY?!
OWW! WHY'D YOU DO THAT?
YOU TOLD ME TO.

THAT IS ONE OF THE MISSION PARAMETERS.
COOL! MY OWN TERMINATOR!
I'M GONNA GO GET MY MOM.

YOU'RE COMING WITH ME!

1984. YOU WERE THERE. HE KILLED SEVENTEEN POLICE OFFICERS THAT NIGHT. RECOGNIZE HIM?
THE SECOND WAS TAKEN TODAY.
MS. CONNOR, YOUR SON'S MISSING. HIS FOSTER PARENTS ARE MURDERED, AND WE KNOW THIS GUY'S INVOLVED. TALK TO US!
DON'T YOU CARE!
WE'RE WASTING OUR TIME.
SORRY, GENTLEMEN...
DOUGLAS, PLEASE TAKE HER BACK TO HER ROOM.
UHHNN... USE THE PAPER CLIP LIKE YOU LEARNED...
NEARBY...
LISTEN CAREFULLY. YOU CAN'T KILL ANYBODY ANYMORE. GOT IT?
WHY?
WHATTAYA MEAN, WHY?! YOU JUST CAN'T! TRUST ME ON THIS!
BE OUT OF THIS CAGE SOON...

YEAH, GO ON.
PESCADERO HOSPIT
TAP TAP
KRAK
AIN'T NO TROUBLE AT ALL!
YOU HAVE A SARAH CONNOR HERE?
RUNNING LATE, AREN'T YOU? YOUR FRIENDS ARE ON THEIR WAY OUT...
WHERE...?
LEWIS, SEE THESE GENTLEMEN OUT AND THEN LOCK UP FOR THE NIGHT.
GOODNIGHT.
SSSLLLUUUPP
OH, MY GOD!

...TO MAKE SURE THE THORAZINE IS ADMINISTERED...
SARAH CONNOR
CELL
#19

SARAH?!
I'M SAVING YOUR MISERABLE LIFE, TOO!
WAPWAPWAP
ALARM
THERE'S 205 BONES IN THE HUMAN BODY, YOU GEEK. THAT'S ONE.
NOW DON'T MOVE! I MEAN IT!
FIGURES THEY'D LOCK IT UP. INMATES'D PROBABLY DRINK IT--
LIQUID ROOTER
HEY, DOC, HOW'D YOU LIKE A LIQUID ROOTER INJECTION?

NOW REMEMBER, YOU'RE NOT GOING TO KILL ANYONE, RIGHT?
RIGHT.
SWEAR.
WHAT?
JUST SWEAR YOU WON'T KILL ANYONE!
I SWEAR I WON'T KILL ANYONE.

OKAY, GUYS, WHAT'S YOUR DEAL?
SSKREEEEEE

YOU GOTTA--
BLAM!
ARRRRGG!
YOU SWORE--
HE'LL LIVE.

THERE'S NO WAY, CONNOR. LET THE DOCTOR GO.
OPEN IT OR HE'LL BE DEAD BEFORE HE HITS THE FLOOR!
YOU'RE NO KILLER, SARAH. I DON'T BELIEVE YOU'D DO IT!

YOU'RE ALREADY DEAD, SILBERMAN. EVERYBODY HERE DIES! YOU KNOW I BELIEVE THAT! SO DON'T JERK ME AROUND!
O-OPEN THE BLASTED DOOR!
STEP BACK!
KRAK
GAAAK!
YOU'RE ALL DEAD!

GET HER!
AROOOOO
AROOOOO
AROOOOO

WE GOT YOU NOW, BABY!
C'MON! OPEN!
KA-KUNK
ELEVATORS!
SLAM!
AROOO AROOOO
NO! NOT YOU--
NOOOOO...!
MOM! WAIT!

JOHN?
OOOOF!
NO! HELP ME! IT'S GOING TO KILL US ALL!
RELAX, SARAH!
HUUULLPH!
WHAMMPCH
SKEESHH
Y-Y-YOU CAN'T BE H-HUMAN--
WHAMM
MOM? ARE YOU OKAY?
COME WITH ME IF YOU WANT TO LIVE.
IT'S ALL RIGHT, MOM. THIS TERMINATOR'S HERE TO HELP.

CHECK OUT THAT COP-- SOMETHING'S WEIRD ABOUT HIM!
GET BEHIND ME, JOHN!
SSHHHUUIIPPPP!!
GO! RUN!
KPOW! KPOW! KPOW! KPOW!
WUP
WUP WUP
BWOOM BWOOM BWOOM
KPOW! KPOW! KLIK KLIK

GOTTA GET TO THE GARAGE!
GEEZ!
SSWWIK!
BWOOM!

AWESOME!

CHUNG!

WHANG
WHUD!
CHK
SHAK
SSWNIKK
BLAM!
BLAM!
BWOOM
BLAM
BLAM
B L 1
C'MON!!
SECURE TRANSPORTATION!
BWOOM
BWOOM
BWOOM

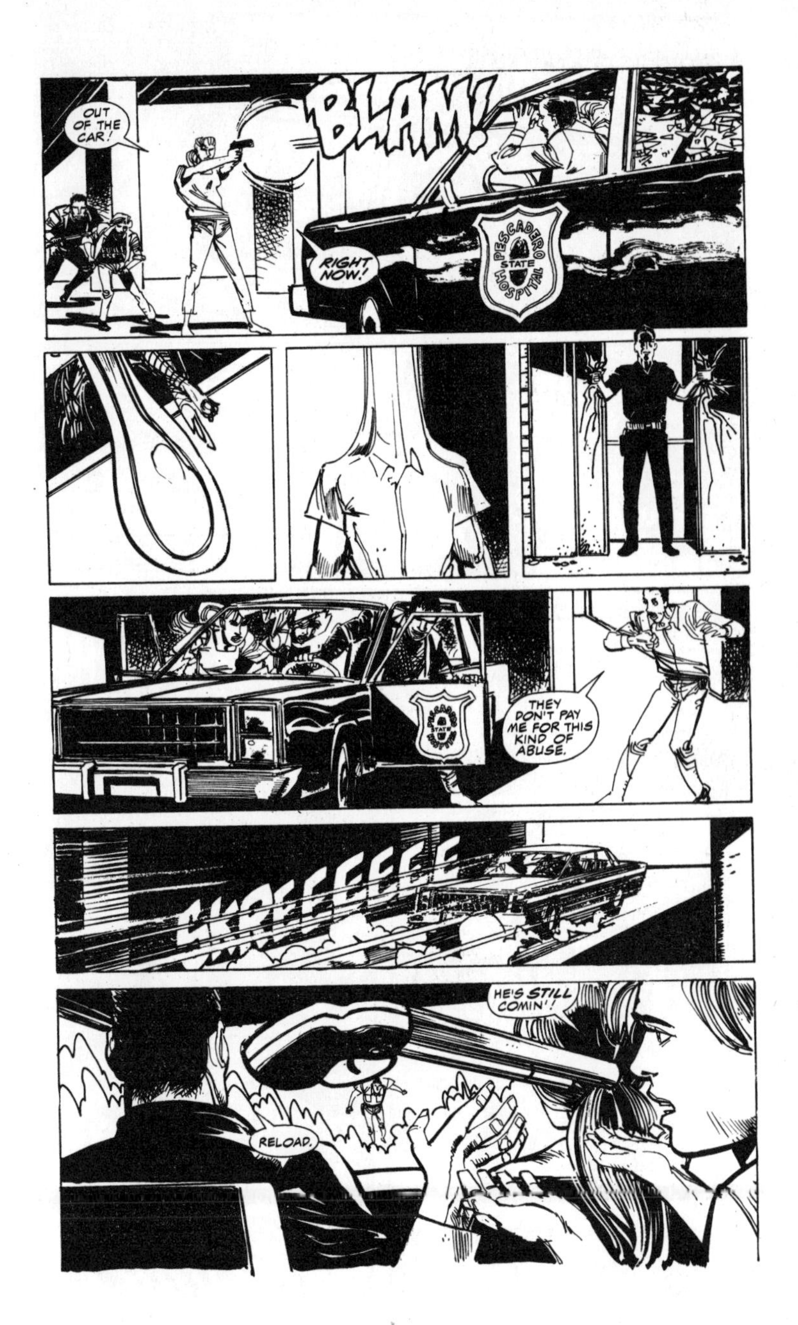
OUT OF THE CAR!
BLAM!
RIGHT NOW!
PESCADERO STATE HOSPITAL
THEY DON'T PAY ME FOR THIS KIND OF ABUSE.
SKREEEEEEE
HE'S STILL COMIN'!
RELOAD.

VRRRRMMM
HERE!
HANG ON!
BWOOM!
FWAAM
ENTRANCE
SKREEEE
WUNK!
WE GOT COMPANY!

KREESH!
WHOAH!
BWOOM!
SPLATCH

WHEW!
I DON'T THINK IT'S DEAD YET.
SHHLLP

VRRRRRRRRRRR

CAN YOU SEE ANYTHING WITH THE LIGHTS OUT?

EVERYTHING.
COOL.
YOU OKAY?
AYE-FIRMATIVE.
NOTHING BROKEN...

I SAID I WAS OKAY!

IT WAS STUPID OF YOU TO GO THERE.
JOHN, YOU HAVE TO BE SMARTER THAN THAT. YOU'RE TOO IMPORTANT! YOU CAN'T RISK YOURSELF, NOT EVEN FOR ME!
YOU UNDERSTAND?!
I... I HAD TO GET YOU OUT... I'M SORRY... I...
STOP IT! YOU CAN'T CRY, JOHN! OTHER KIDS CAN AFFORD TO CRY. YOU CAN'T.
WHAT'S WRONG WITH YOUR EYES?
nothin'.
SO WHAT'S YOUR STORY?
LATER...
CLOSED
THIS T-1000... WHAT HAPPENS WHEN YOU SHOOT IT?
BALLISTIC PENETRATION SHOCKS IT, BUT ONLY FOR A FEW SECONDS.
CAN IT BE DESTROYED?
UNKNOWN.

SHORTLY...
WILL THESE HEAL UP?
YES.
GOOD. IF YOU CAN'T PASS FOR HUMAN, YOU'RE NO GOOD TO US.
HOW LONG DO YOU LIVE, I MEAN LAST?
A HUNDRED AND TWENTY YEARS ON MY EXISTING POWER CELL.
HUH. CAN YOU LEARN? SO YOU CAN BE... YOU KNOW, MORE HUMAN.
MY CPU IS A NEURAL NET PROCESSOR... A LEARNING COMPUTER. BUT SKYNET PRESETS THE SWITCH TO "READ ONLY."
DOESN'T WANT YOU THINKING TOO MUCH, HUH?
NO.
CAN WE RESET THE SWITCH?
AND SO...
NOW OPEN THE PORT COVER.
HOLD THE CPU BY ITS BASE TAB. PULL.
RADICAL. TERMINATOR BRAIN!
WHOAH. NOBODY HOME. CAN YOU SEE THE PIN SWITCH?

NO!

OUT OF THE WAY, JOHN.
NO! DON'T KILL *HIM*.
IT, JOHN. NOT *HIM*. *IT!*

ALL RIGHT, *IT*. WE *NEED* IT!
WE'RE BETTER OFF BY OURSELVES.

BUT IT'S THE ONLY *PROOF* WE HAVE OF THE *FUTURE*...
...ABOUT THE WAR AND ALL THAT...
I DON'T *TRUST* IT! THESE THINGS ARE HARD TO KILL-- WE MAY NEVER--
LOOK, MOM, IF I'M SUPPOSED TO BE THIS GREAT *LEADER*, YOU SHOULD START LISTENING TO MY LEADERSHIP IDEAS. 'CAUSE IF YOU DON'T, NOBODY ELSE WILL!

TEK
CHK
WRRMMMMM
WAS THERE A PROBLEM?
NO PROBLEM. NONE WHATSOEVER.

MORNING...
WAK
SHKSHK
VRRMMMM
ARE WE LEARNING YET?
WE NEED TO GET AS FAR FROM THE CITY AS POSSIBLE.
JUST HEAD SOUTH.
KEEP IT UNDER SIXTY-FIVE. WE CAN'T AFFORD TO GET PULLED OVER.
AFFIRMATIVE.
NO, NO, NO. YOU GOTTA LISTEN TO THE WAY PEOPLE TALK.
SEE, YOU DON'T SAY "AFFIRMITIVE" OR SOME JUNK LIKE THAT. YOU SAY... "NO PROBLEMO."
IF SOMEONE COMES OFF TO YOU WITH ATTITUDE, YOU SAY, "STICK IT"...
IF YOU WANT TO SHINE THEM ON, IT'S "HASTA LA VISTA, BABY."
HASTA LA VISTA, BABY?
YEAH, OR "LATER JERKWAD" OR IF SOMEONE GETS UPSET, YOU SAY, "CHILL OUT."
OR YOU CAN DO COMBINATIONS.
CHILL OUT, JERKWAD.
NO PROBLEMO.
THAT'S GREAT! NOW YOU'RE GETTING IT.

THAT AFTERNOON...
ALSO, YOU GOTTA LEARN TO SMILE. YOU KNOW? PEOPLE SMILE, RIGHT? WATCH.
LIKE THIS.

MAYBE YOU COULD PRACTICE IN FRONT OF A MIRROR.

I NEED TO KNOW HOW SKYNET GETS BUILT. WHO'S RESPONSIBLE?
THE MAN MOST DIRECTLY RESPONSIBLE IS MILES BENNET DYSON, DIRECTOR OF SPECIAL PROJECTS AT CYBERDYNE SYSTEMS CORPORATION.

WHY HIM?
IN A FEW MONTHS HE CREATES A REVOLUTIONARY TYPE OF MICROPROCESSOR.
IN THREE YEARS CYBERDYNE WILL BECOME THE LARGEST SUPPLIER OF MILITARY COMPUTER SYSTEMS.
THEN WHAT?
GREAT. THEN THOSE FAT JACKALS IN WASHINGTON FIGURE, "LET A COMPUTER RUN THE WHOLE SHOW," RIGHT?
BASICALLY. THE SYSTEM GOES ONLINE AUGUST 4TH, 1997. HUMAN DECISIONS ARE REMOVED FROM STRATEGIC DEFENSE. SKYNET BEGINS TO LEARN, AT A GEOMETRIC RATE.

IT BECOMES SELF-AWARE AT 2:14 A.M. EASTERN STANDARD TIME, AUGUST 29TH.
IN A PANIC, THEY TRY TO PULL THE PLUG.
AND SKYNET FIGHTS BACK, CAUSING A NUCLEAR HOLOCAUST.
IT SUCCEEDED IN ELIMINATING ITS ENEMIES.
MY GOD.
HOW MUCH DO YOU KNOW ABOUT DYSON?
I HAVE DETAILED FILES.

"I WANT TO KNOW EVERYTHING. WHAT HE LOOKS LIKE. WHERE HE LIVES. EVERYTHING."
MILES, IT'S SUNDAY. YOU PROMISED TO TAKE THE KIDS TO RAGING WATERS TODAY.
OH. I CAN'T, HONEY. I'M ON A ROLL HERE.

BABY, THIS THING IS GOING TO BLOW 'EM ALL AWAY. IT'S A--
I KNOW. YOU TOLD ME. IT'S A NEURAL-NET PROCESSOR. IT THINKS AND LEARNS LIKE WE DO. OTHER COMPUTERS ARE POCKET CALCULATORS IN COMPARISON.
BUT WHY IS THAT SO IMPORTANT, MILES? I REALLY NEED TO KNOW, 'CAUSE I FEEL LIKE I'M GOING CRAZY HERE, SOMETIMES.
I'M SORRY, HONEY, IT'S JUST THAT I'M THIIIIIS CLOSE.
WHY DID YOU MARRY ME, MILES? WHY DID WE HAVE THESE CHILDREN? YOU DON'T NEED US!

YOUR HEART AND MIND ARE IN HERE, IN THIS COMPUTER, BUT IT DOESN'T LOVE YOU LIKE WE DO
I'M SORRY.

HOW ABOUT SPENDING SOME TIME WITH YOUR OTHER BABIES?
ABSOLUTELY.

CHARON MESA, IN THE DESERT. NEAR THE MEXICAN BORDER.
<HE'S COOL, ENRIQUE! HE'S... UH... THIS IS MY UNCLE BOB!>
<GOOD TO SEE YOU, CONNOR. I KNEW YOU'D MAKE IT BACK HERE SOONER OR LATER.>
UNCLE BOB, THIS IS ENRIQUE.
OYE, BIG JOHN! QUÉ PASA? WHO'S YOUR VERY LARGE FRIEND?
HMM. UNCLE BOB, HUH? OKAY.
I JUST CAME FOR MY STUFF. AND I NEED CLOTHES, FOOD, AND ONE OF YOUR TRUCKS.
SO, SARAHLITA, YOU GETTING FAMOUS, YOU KNOW THAT? ALL OVER THE TV.
HEY, HOW ABOUT THE FILLINGS OUT OF MY TEETH WHILE YOU'RE AT IT?
NOW, ENRIQUE!
?
YOU TWO ARE ON WEAPONS DETAIL.
ONE THING ABOUT MY MOM...

...SHE ALWAYS PLANS AHEAD.
EXCELLENT.
YEAH. I THOUGHT YOU'D LIKE THIS PLACE.
THIS IS THE BEST TRUCK.
IT'S TOO DANGEROUS FOR YOU HERE. YOU GET OUT TONIGHT TOO, OKAY?
YEAH, SARAHLITA, SURE. DROP BY ANY-TIME AND TOTALLY SCREW UP MY LIFE!
ARE YOU EVER AFRAID OF DYING?
NO. I HAVE TO STAY FUNCTIONAL UNTIL MY MISSION IS COMPLETE. THEN IT DOESN'T MATTER.
YEAH. I HAVE TO STAY FUNCTIONAL, TOO. I'M "TOO IMPORTANT."
IT'S DEFINITELY YOU.
THERE WAS THIS ONE GUY MOM WAS WITH WHO WAS COOL. HE TAUGHT ME ENGINES. MOM SCREWED IT UP, OF COURSE.
SHE'D MENTION JUDGMENT DAY AND ME BEING THIS GREAT LEADER, AND THAT'D BE ALL SHE WROTE.
TORQUE WRENCH, PLEASE.

HERE. I WISH I COULDA MET MY REAL DAD.
YOU WILL.

YEAH. I GUESS SO. MOM SAYS WHEN I'M LIKE, 45, I SEND HIM BACK THROUGH TIME.

"MOM AND HIM WERE ONLY TOGETHER FOR ONE NIGHT, BUT SHE STILL LOVES HIM I GUESS."

VRRRRMMM
ALL RIGHT! MY MAN!
NO PROBLEMO.

MEANWHILE...

...IF WE EVER GET SEPARATED AND CAN'T MAKE CONTACT, GO TO ENRIQUE'S AIRSTRIP. I'LL RENDEZVOUS WITH YOU THERE.
CHARON MESA, CA
HOWDY. I SAW YOU PULLED OVER HERE EARLIER.

CHARON
MESA,
CA
EVERYTHING OKAY?

EVERYTHING'S FINE. THANKS FOR CHECKING. SINCE YOU'RE HERE, THOUGH, CAN I TALK TO YOU A SECOND...

OF ALL THE WOULD-BE FATHERS WHO CAME AND WENT OVER THE YEARS, THIS THING, THIS TERMINATOR, WAS THE ONLY ONE WHO MEASURED UP.
IT WOULD NEVER LEAVE HIM. IT WOULD NEVER HURT HIM. IT WAS THE SANEST CHOICE.
ESPECIALLY WITH WHAT I HAD TO DO.

SHE SAID YOU GO SOUTH WITH HIM ...TONIGHT, LIKE YOU PLANNED. SHE WILL MEET YOU TOMORROW IN...
WHY DIDN'T YOU STOP HER?

"NO FATE." MY FATHER TOLD HER THIS... I MADE HIM MEMORIZE--
NO FATE
"THE FUTURE IS NOT SET. THERE IS NO FATE BUT WHAT WE MAKE FOR OURSELVES."
SHE INTENDS TO CHANGE THE FUTURE SOMEHOW.

I GUESS, YEAH... OH, GEEZ!

DYSON.

YEAH, GOTTA BE! MILES DYSON. SHE'S GONNA BLOW HIM AWAY!

C'MON, LET'S GO!

THIS IS TACTICALLY DANGEROUS.
THE T-1000 HAS THE SAME FILES THAT I DO. IT COULD ANTICIPATE THIS MOVE AND TRY TO REACQUIRE YOU AT DYSON'S HOUSE.
I DON'T CARE. WE'VE GOTTA STOP HER.
KILLING DYSON MIGHT ACTUALLY PREVENT THE WAR.
I DON'T CARE! THERE'S GOTTA BE ANOTHER WAY! HAVEN'T YOU LEARNED ANYTHING? HAVEN'T YOU FIGURED OUT WHY YOU CAN'T KILL PEOPLE?
"LOOK, MAYBE YOU DON'T CARE IF YOU LIVE OR DIE, BUT EVERYBODY'S NOT LIKE THAT. OKAY?! WE HAVE FEELINGS. WE HURT. WE'RE AFRAID.
"YOU GOTTA LEARN THIS STUFF, MAN. I'M NOT KIDDING. IT'S IMPORTANT!"
WAP!
PFFT!

CHOOMCHOOMCHOOM
NEVER MAKE IT TO THE DOOR ALIVE...
RUN, KIDS! GO! RUN!!
BLAM BLAM
AHHRRR!
PLEASE... LET... THE KIDS... GO...
SHUT UP! SHUT UP, TRAITOR! IT'S ALL YOUR FAULT!
DAAAAADDDDEEE!
DANNY!
DON'T MOVE! ON THE FLOOR, RIGHT NOW!
DON'T YOU HURT MY DADDY!
...YOUR FAULT...
MOM! YOU OKAY?
I COULDN'T ...OH, GOD.
YOU... CAME HERE... TO STOP ME?
UH HUH.

IT'S OKAY. WE'LL FIGURE IT OUT.
I LOVE YOU, JOHN. I ALWAYS HAVE.
I KNOW, MOM. I KNOW.

IT'S ONLY A FLESH WOUND.
WH-WHO ARE YOU PEOPLE?
SHOW HIM.

MY GOD...
NOW LISTEN CAREFULLY...

TERMINATOR LAID IT ALL DOWN. SKY-NET. JUDGMENT DAY. THE HISTORY OF THINGS TO COME.
IT'S NOT EVERY DAY YOU FIND OUT YOU'RE RESPONSIBLE FOR 3 BILLION DEATHS.
I THINK I'M GONNA THROW UP.
THERE'S NO WAY I'M GOING TO FINISH THE NEW PROCESSOR NOW. FORGET IT... I'M OUT. I'M QUITTING CYBERDYNE--
THAT'S NOT GOOD ENOUGH!
"YOU'RE RIGHT. WE HAVE TO DESTROY THE STUFF AT THE LAB, THE FILES, DISK DRIVES... AND EVERYTHING I HAVE HERE..."

DO YOU KNOW ABOUT THE OTHER CHIP, SARAH?
WHAT CHIP?
THEY HAVE IT AT CYBERDYNE... IT'S GOTTA BE FROM THE OTHER ONE LIKE HIM.
THE CPU FROM THE FIRST TERMINATOR.
THE BRAIN ...I KNEW IT!
ALL OUR WORK IS BASED ON IT.
"CAN YOU GET US INTO CYBERDYNE, PAST SECURITY?"
EVENING, PAUL. I JUST THOUGHT I'D TAKE MY FRIENDS FROM OUT OF TOWN UP FOR A LOOK--
SORRY, MR. DYSON. YOU KNOW THE RULES ABOUT VISITORS IN THE LAB. I NEED WRITTEN--
I INSIST.
DON'T EVEN THINK ABOUT THE ALARM. JOHN --LOSE HIM!
THE VAULT NEEDS TWO KEYS TO OPEN. MINE...
...AND THE ONE FROM THE SECURITY STATION. I CAN GET THE OTHER KEY FROM THE SAFE.

PAUL, I FINISHED--AW HEY MAN, WHERE THE--

YOU SHOULDN'T GO TO THE CAN AND LEAVE-- UH OH!

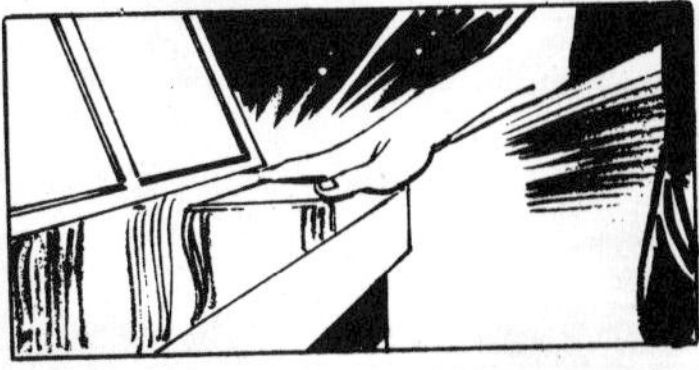

WHAT? WHY WON'T IT OPEN?
SILENT ALARM'S BEEN TRIPPED. CODES THROUGHOUT THE BUILDING ARE NEUTRALIZED. NOTHING'LL OPEN.

WE HAVE TO ABORT THE MISSION

YOU GUYS GET STARTED ON THE LAB. I CAN OPEN THIS!

SECONDS LATER...
MY KEY DOESN'T WORK.
LET ME TRY.

KWA BOOM

WE'RE REALLY GOING TO DO IT...

INTERIOR, DYSON HOUSE.
ALL UNITS, 211 IN PROGRESS AT 2144 KRAMER STREET, THE CYBERDYNE BUILDING. MULTIPLE SUSPECTS, ARMED WITH AUTOMATIC WEAPONS AND EXPLOSIVES...

SWAT UNIT IS EN ROUTE...

BACK AT THE LAB.
YEAH, ALL THAT STUFF! AND ALL THE DISKS IN THOSE OF-FICES-- MY OFFICE, ESPECIALLY!
THESE TOO! YEAH. AND ALL THIS HERE...
GIVE ME THAT THING A SECOND.
I WORKED FOR YEARS ON THIS STUFF!
EASY MONEY.
HOW DO YOU SET THEM OFF?
RADIO REMOTE.
EXTERIOR, CYBERDYNE BUILDING.
THIS IS SWAT LEADER. WE'RE GOING IN.
I'D LIKE TO SEE THEM TRY TO GET OUT OF THIS!

LET'S SEE WHAT'S BEHIND DOOR NUMBER ONE!
HERE'S THE ARM, AND YOU'RE HOLDING THE PROCESSOR.
GOT OL' SKYNET BY THE BRASS NOW, MILES. COME ON, LET'S BOOK!
READY TO ROCK?
TIME TO GO. RIGHT NOW!
DYSON, HAND ME THE DETONATOR! LET'S GO!
BRAKKA
BRAKKABRAKKA
AEEII!
MOMMM!
GO...
BRAKKABRAK

CHAM! CHAM! CHAM!
COME ON!
I DON'T KNOW...HOW MUCH LONGER ...I CAN...HOLD THIS DETON-ATOR...
FALL BACK! NOW!
KOFF KOFF JOHN! KOFF HURRY!
GOODBYE...
KLIK
KAVOOM!

DON'T FORGET, IT'S ALWAYS DARKEST BEFORE ...YOU'RE TOTALLY SCREWED.
KEEP YOUR EYES CLOSED. DON'T MOVE.
I'LL BE BACK.

HOW'S HE HANDLING THE TEAR GAS?
FACE DOWN ON THE FLOOR! NOW!

DROP HIM!
BRAKKABRAKKABRAKKA
YOU'RE NOT HITTING HIM!

YES I AM!
BLAM
BLAM
AARGH-- MY LEG!

WHAT IS THIS THING?!

UHHH!
PSSHHT...
PSSHHT
HEY MAN--
WHOAAA!
LATER, JERKWAD.
SKKKREESH!!!
SKREEEEEEEE
SORRY, LOVE TO STAY, BUT...
JOHN!

HOLY--
VRRRRSKKASHHH
VUK VUK VUK
GET UNDER THESE!
WHOOA! DID YOU SEE--
HANG ON!
I DON'T QUIT EITHER--
AHHRRR!
BRAKKA BRAKKA
KKKRRUNKKT
SKREEEEEEEEEE
RADICAL. YOU OKAY?
FOR NOW...

HOLD ON. THE VAN LOST A TIRE!
FOOM!

MOMMMM!
SKKKSSSHHH

SAY--ARE YOU ALRIGHT, FRIEND?
LIQUID NITROGEN CRYOCO
THAT WAS--
ULLLPHH!
NEED SOME HELP?
HE'S *STILL* COMING! MOM, WE GOTTA KEEP MOVING!
WE NEED YOUR TRUCK.

SMAASHH

FASTER! HE'S RIGHT ON US!

SHREEEE
FWANNCK!

DRIVE FOR A MINUTE.
AND WHERE ARE YOU GOING?
BWOOM!

BILL RD
EXIT ¼ MILE

FWAMMM
STEEL INDUSTRIES
HANG ON, MOM!
LIQUID NITROGEN
WHAMMPCH
LET'S GET OUT OF HERE!
LOOK!...
...THE LIQUID NITROGEN IS FREEZING IT!
CLINK
SSS
CLINK
SSS

HASTA LA VISTA, BABY.
BLAMM
PAASHHHH
OKAY, MOM, WE GOTTA GET OUT NOW, COME ON.
WE DON'T HAVE MUCH TIME.
WHAT?! BUT YOU JUST SHATTERED THAT POPSICLE--
YOU GOTTA BE YANKIN' MY--
COME ON, MOM!
RUN FOR IT!

KEEP GOING!
RUN!
LET'S GO, MOM!
WAK
WHUMP
SHHLLP

SPLATCH
STAY AWAY FROM MY SON!
KPOW
CALL TO JOHN. NOW.
SSSHK
RRRUNCH
SPLUTCH
SMAKK
CHUNK
ZZDAT
ZZDAT
ZZDAT

JOHN? JOHN? CAN YOU HEAR ME?
WHERE ARE YOU?
MOM?
HELP ME, HONEY...
GET OUT OF THE WAY, JOHN.
WHICH--
SHOOT!!!
BWOOM BWOOM BWOOM
YOU'RE TERMINATED, YOU MERCURY MOTHER--
KLIK
EMPTY...? NO!

CHK
EAT THIS, JERKWAD.
PSHHT
"HAVE A NICE SWIM IN THE MOLTEN STEEL.
SPLUTCH
"TERMINATED."
WILL IT MELT IN THERE?
YES. THROW IT IN.
AND THE CHIP.
IT'S FINALLY OVER.
NO. THERE IS ANOTHER CHIP...

...IN HERE.
NO!

I HAVE TO GO AWAY JOHN. IT MUST END HERE... OR I AM THE FUTURE.
DON'T DO IT. PLEASE ...DON'T GO...

I KNOW NOW WHY YOU CRY, THOUGH IT IS SOMETHING I CAN NEVER DO.
GOODBYE.

ARE YOU AFRAID?
YES.

THE UNKNOWN FUTURE ROLLS TOWARD US. I FACE IT FOR THE FIRST TIME WITH A SENSE OF HOPE. BECAUSE IF A MACHINE, A TERMINATOR, CAN LEARN THE VALUE OF HUMAN LIFE, MAYBE WE CAN TOO.

TERMINATOR 2®
CYBERNETIC DAWN

SCRIPT BY
DAN ABNETT

STORY BY
DAN ABNETT & MARK PANICCIA
WITH GERRY KLINE

ART BY
ROD WHIGHAM
AND JACK SNIDER

BASED ON THE WORLD CREATED
IN THE MOTION PICTURE WRITTEN BY
JAMES CAMERON AND WILLIAM WISHER

LOST & FOUND
DAN ABNETT • script
ROD WHIGHAM • penciller
JACK SNIDER • inker
DAVE LANPHEAR • letterer
MOOSE BAUMANN • color design
MALIBU • interior color
DAN SHAHEEN • editor
MARK PANICCIA • media line editor
cover by ROB PRIOR
story by DAN ABNETT & MARK PANICCIA with GERRY KLINE
TERMINATOR 2: JUDGMENT DAY
The Machines were our legacy, and our curse.
On August 29, 1997, they out-evolved us in the blink of an eye, and set about manufacturing our extinction.
But they underestimated humanity's resolve. They underestimated it then, and they underestimate it now.
Even when they resorted to time travel in a bid to erase our species...
...the Machines lost. Their future was crushed in a steel-press.
Their future melted in a blast-furnace.
I never asked for the responsibility of preserving mankind. It was forced on me, one night in nineteen eighty four, in a Los Angeles club called Tech Noir.
A voice said, "Come with me if you want to live," and my life as Sarah Connor, waitress, ended.

And my responsibilities began. Thirteen years before the eve of war. I've been fighting ever since.
Fighting for John, my only son. The human that the machines fear most of all.
The human who will defeat them.
They tried to kill him once, by killing me, before he was born. That was when I heard the voice.
It belonged to KYLE REESE. Voluntarily, he tumbled back through the years to protect me.
I will always love him. I see his scarred, noble beauty in John's face all the time.
And then tonight, ten years AFTER Kyle, the Machines struck again.
This time as a fluid thing. A shapechanger.
Together, John and I denied it. This time we fought alongside one of the machines, a re-programmed device that the adult John Connor, in years to come, would send back to safeguard our lives.
The thing I dread above all else.
A TERMINATOR.
Now dawn comes up and we've run as far as we can go.
I want to sleep. I want to sleep forever.
Enrique Salceda, Desert Gypsy, is an old ally.
He's sheltered me before. I pray he'll do it again.

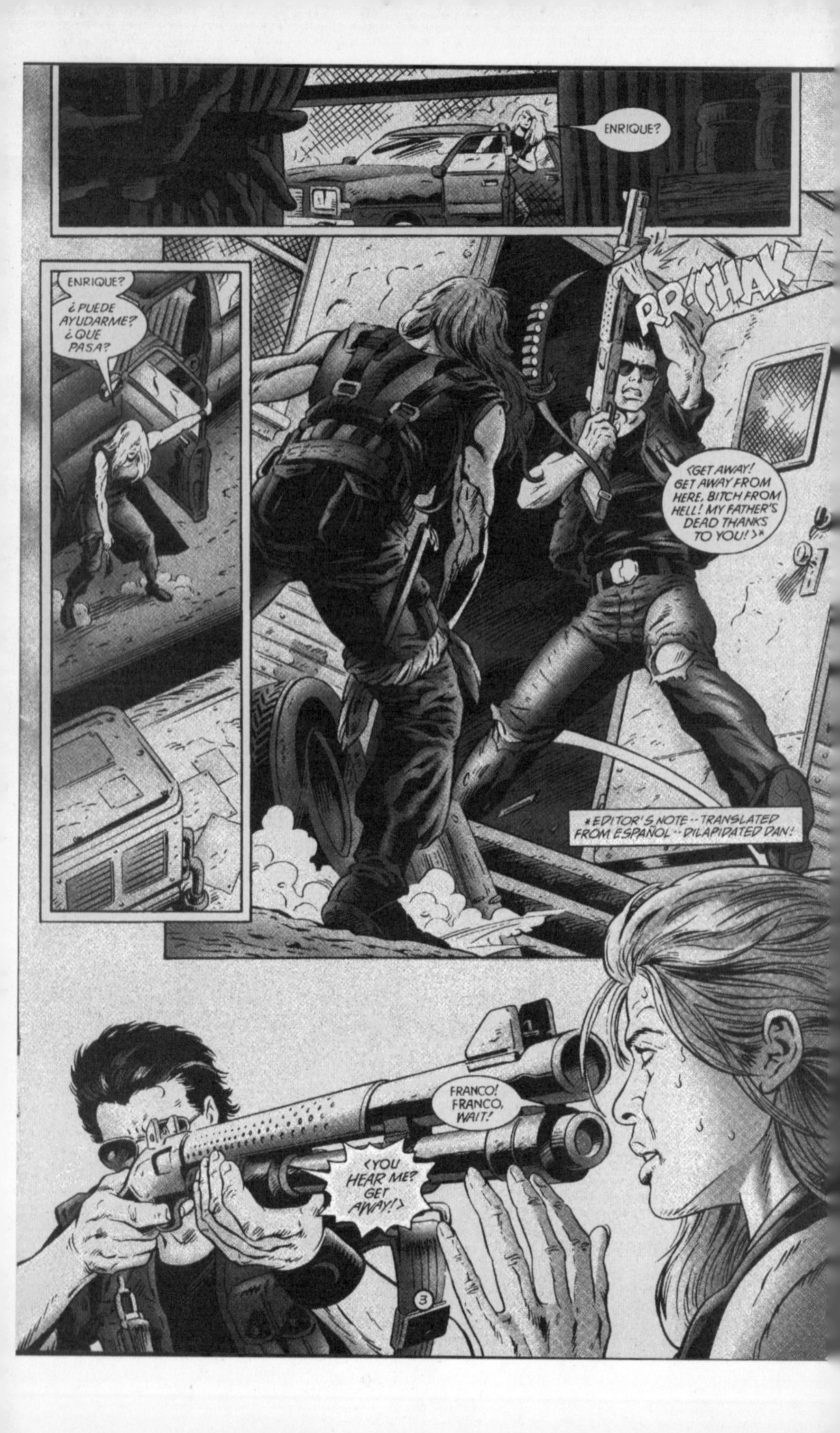
ENRIQUE?
ENRIQUE?
¿PUEDE AYUDARME? ¿QUE PASA?
RR-CHAK
<GET AWAY! GET AWAY FROM HERE, BITCH FROM HELL! MY FATHER'S DEAD THANKS TO YOU!>*
*EDITOR'S NOTE--TRANSLATED FROM ESPAÑOL--DILAPIDATED DAN!
FRANCO! FRANCO, WAIT!
<YOU HEAR ME? GET AWAY!>
3

DROP IT, DICKWAD! CHILL OUT OR I SMOKE YOUR TEX-MEX ASS!
JOHN! NO!
WHAT THE HELL?
NO, JOHN, D--
...UGHNNN!
M-MOM?
MOM!
M-MOM?
LO SIENTO, CHICO...
...I THINK SHE'S DEAD.

I hear the voice.
HIS voice.
DO YOU WANT TO LIVE? DO YOU REALLY WANT TO LIVE?

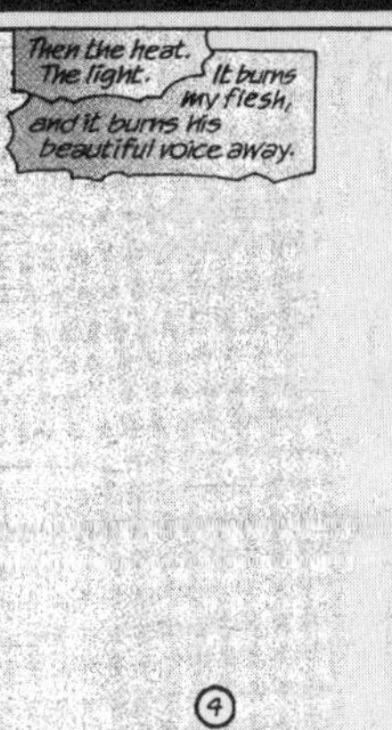
Then the heat. The light.
It burns my flesh, and it burns his beautiful voice away.

I want to cry, but my tears evaporate in the heat burst.
I know what this is. I KNOW WHAT THIS IS.

And then...
SARAH.
I CAME BACK ACROSS TIME FOR YOU.
I LOVE YOU. I ALWAYS HAVE.
KYLE!
IT HURTS. IT HURTS SO MUCH.
PAIN CAN BE CONTROLLED. YOU DISCONNECT IT.
I TOLD YOU THAT.
I HAD A PICTURE OF YOU.
I MEMORIZED EVERY LINE, EVERY CURVE...
...SO THAT I WOULD NOT MISTAKE YOU WHEN I FOUND YOU.
KYLE?
AHH!
NOOO!

SARAH CONNOR?
GET AWAY FROM ME!
GET AWAY FROM ME, YOU SON OF A BITCH!

Oh, GOD, PLEASE... NO MORE...
...NOT AGAIN... NOT AGAIN...

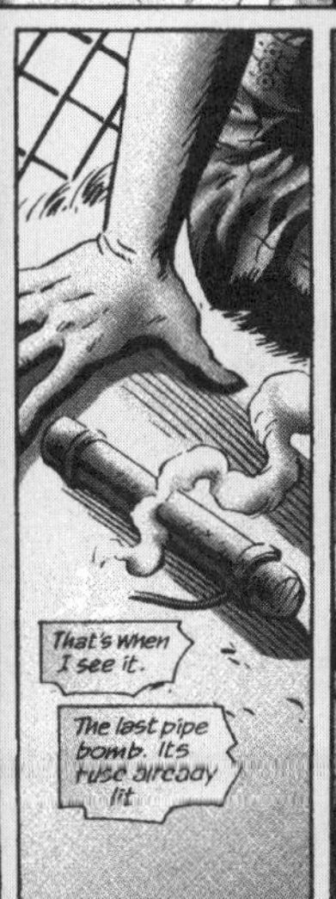
That's when I see it.
The last pipe bomb. Its fuse already lit.

SARAH?
NO! NO! NOOO!

THE FUTURE IS NOT SET. THERE'S NO FATE BUT WHAT WE MAKE FOR OURSELVES.
YOU KNOW THAT, SARAH CONNOR. SO WHY DID YOU HAVE TO KILL ME?
DYSON? DYSON?!

FSSZZ

NUUUH!
...oh. MAN.
YEAH, JUST LIKE THAT. LIKE SOME DEVIL.
MOM!
I'M OKAY.
FRANCO. I'M SORRY ABOUT YOUR FATHER.
WHAT IS IT YOU HAVE BROUGHT INTO THIS WORLD, CONNOR?
I don't know how to answer him. I listen as he tells me about Enrique, in a voice as dry as the desert...
...the motorcycle cop who rode in out of the night.
Who shrugged off bullets, and pinned his father to an ammo crate with a finger made from razor blades.
Who asked about John Connor.

He tells me about the curse Enrique spat...
...and the grenade.
And the blast that followed.
And the way the devil-cop stepped from the fire...
...and REASSEMBLED himself.
The polyalloy T-1000.
It came here looking for John and me, and
rather than betray us.

So it turned on the children...
...it didn't kill them. It just asked them which way we went.
They didn't know any better. They were just scared. They pointed down the road.
AND THEN, IT THANKED US AND RODE AWAY.
CAN YOU BELIEVE THAT? IT THANKED US?
There's so much pain here, so much pain wherever I go.
Touching families, tearing them apart.
The Dysons, the Salcedas, the Voights, the Connors.
Sometimes I ask myself if it's worth going on.
Last night may have been the end, but I can't be sure.
And because I can't be sure, we'll never be safe. Not while there is a chance that SKYNET will still be born.
John and I are doomed to be victims, fugitives, outlaws... forever running, forever watching our backs and jumping at shadows.
And touching everyone we meet with our curse.
9

STEEL MILL, WILMINGTON.
...DETECTIVE WEATHERBY, L.A.P.D.
CAN YOU TELL ME WHAT'S GOING ON?
CSI STEEL
I'M AFRAID THIS MATTER IS NOW UNDER FEDERAL JURISDICTION, DETECTIVE. WHAT'S YOUR INTEREST HERE?
WE'RE LOOKING FOR AN ESCAPEE FROM PESCADERO, ONE SARAH CONNOR. SHE WAS INVOLVED IN THE FIRE-FIGHT AT CYBERDYNE LAST NIGHT, AND THAT TRAIL LEADS HERE.
FBI
POLICE LINE DO NOT CROSS
WISH I COULD HELP. I'M NOT AT LIBERTY TO COMMENT ON THAT.
YOU AND YOUR PARTNER HAD BETTER BE ON YOUR WAY.
BUT--
GOOD DAY, DETECTIVE.
DON'T TELL ME... THE FEDS AREN'T PLAYING NICE.
WHAT ARE WE SUPPOSED TO DO? FORGET IT?
THIS STINKS, MAN. I WANNA KNOW WHAT THEY'VE GOT IN THERE.
WITH ANY LUCK, IT'S THAT PSYCHO CONNOR IN A BODY BAG.
HEY, HEADS UP. CHECK OUT THE BABE.
SPASKY? I CAME AS FAST AS I COULD.
SORRY TO RUIN YOUR WEEKEND, KARYN, BUT YOU DO NOT WANT TO MISS THIS.
WHAT ARE YOU DOING?
IMPROVISING, BUDDY. GET READY TO MAKE THE MOST OF IT.

HEY, LADY! MAYBE YOU CAN HELP HERE. MOSSBERG, L.A.P.D.
WE MAY BE THE LITTLE GUYS, BUT WE DON'T INTEND TO STAND HERE FREEZING OUR NUTS OFF WHILE YOU GET TO HAVE ALL THE FUN!
I'M SORRY?
Oh, NOT AGAIN.
DETECTIVE, I TOLD YOUR PARTNER THIS WAS OUT OF YOUR JURIS-DICTION...
US 317
CAREFUL, FEDS. DON'T GET HIM STARTED...
POLICE
...CAN YOU GET IT FREE?
GONNA TAKE SOME WORK. WHAT DID SPASKY SAY?
HE SAID WE SHOULD LIFT THE WHEEL RIGHT OUT, SO WE DON'T DAMAGE IT ANY FURTHER.
Oh, SURE...
Oh, MY GOD...

POLICE LINE
DO NOT CROSS
WHAT THE HELL IS THAT?
DETECTIVE WEATHERBY. DID YOU REALLY THINK WE WOULDN'T SEE THROUGH YOUR PARTNER'S TRANSPARENT ATTEMPTS AT DISTRACTING US?
ESCORT HIM FROM THE BUILDING.
NOW WAIT A MINUTE...
YOU'RE LEAVING, MISTER.
AND I SUGGEST YOU REMEMBER THAT YOU HAVE SEEN ABSOLUTELY NOTHING HERE TODAY.
MAN! ARE YOU OKAY? WHAT HAPPENED?
WHAT DID YOU SEE? WEATHERBY?
WHAT DID YOU SEE?
DRIVE. JUST DRIVE.

MOM?
IT'S NEARLY TWO. SHOULDN'T WE BE MOVING BY NOW?
FRANCO'S TAKING HIS FAMILY SOUTH. SOME-PLACE NEAR SAUCILLO. ARE WE STILL HEADING FOR THE PLACE IN THE MOUNTAINS?
I GUESS.
SO, WHAT'S UP?
I WAS THINKING ABOUT DYSON. AND HIS FAMILY.
SHE MUST KNOW BY NOW. SHE MUST KNOW HE ISN'T COMING BACK.
YOU'RE NOT GONNA PULL SOME TRIP ON ME NOW, ARE YOU? SOME GUILT RIFF ABOUT THE PEOPLE WHO GET HURT ALONG THE WAY?
COME ON. THE TIME YOU SPENT TELLING ME WE CAN'T AFFORD TO CARE!
BUT IF IT'S OVER? CAN WE AFFORD TO NOW?
YOU WANT TO GO BACK, DON'T YOU? BACK TO SEE THEM.
AND WHAT WOULD YOU SAY TO THAT?
IF IT IS OVER...
...THEN WE SHOULD.

Somehow, I expected him to talk me out of it. As usual, my son surprises me with his insight.
Perhaps that quality is what could make him so important one day.
55
With Franco's help, we pick up another car at a gas station and then say our goodbyes. I doubt we'll ever see the Salcedas again. For their sake, I hope we don't.
Logical strategy demands we go to ground in one of the bolt-holes I've prepped over the last decade.
But to do that would be to admit defeat. I don't want to think like that. I want to believe that last night at the mill, we turned destiny on its head and cast out the future that's been haunting us.
And if we believe that, then we have this hour of grace, a chance to make peace with the others who have shared in this bloodshed.
I NEED to do this. John knows it. I need to face down the ghosts and prove that fighting Skynet hasn't cost me my soul.
D'YOU THINK WE'LL HAVE TO WAIT FOR... YOU KNOW...
...JUDGMENT DAY...
...BEFORE WE'LL KNOW?
YOU MEAN, BEFORE WE KNOW IF WE WON?
I HOPE NOT.
I KNOW THIS MUCH, THOUGH... IF WE DIDN'T WIN...
...WE'LL FIND OUT PRETTY SOON.

SIMI VALLEY, CALIFORNIA.
Ms. STERN? THEY'RE READY FOR YOU.
NetWork DEVELOPMENTS
THANK YOU FOR COMING. I HOPE THE SHORT NOTICE HASN'T FOULED UP YOUR SCHEDULES.
PROCEED, PLEASE, Ms. STERN. I'VE GOT A FOUR THIRTY WITH THE GOVERNOR.
LATE LAST NIGHT, THE CYBERDYNE FACILITY IN IRVINE WAS INFILTRATED AND LEVELLED IN WHAT APPEARS TO HAVE BEEN A TERRORIST ACTION.
THERE WAS EXTENSIVE COLLATERAL DAMAGE AND A LARGE NUMBER OF LAW ENFORCEMENT AGENTS WERE INJURED.
THERE WERE ALSO SEVERAL FATALITIES, INCLUDING CYBER-DYNE PROJECT CHIEF MILES BENNET DYSON.
THE VIOLENCE SPREAD TO THE FREEWAY, AND EVENTUALLY TO A STEEL MILL IN WILMINGTON, WHERE IT APPEARS TO HAVE CONCLUDED.
Mr. SPASKY AND I HAVE JUST RETURNED FROM WILMINGTON. WE MADE A DISCOVERY THERE WHICH WE'LL COME TO IN A MOMENT.
AS YOU KNOW, WE HAVE BEEN WATCHING CYBERDYNE'S RECENT WORK INTENTLY. AS A GOVERNMENT CONTRACTOR, THEY WERE OBLIGED TO PROVIDE THIS OFFICE WITH REGULAR REPORTS.
FROM THERE, WE KNEW THAT DYSON WAS CLOSE TO A GENUINE BREAKTHROUGH ONE THAT WE HAD BEEN KEENLY ANTICIPATING FOR MONTHS.
CLASSIFIED
15

IS THIS YOUR WAY OF BREAKING BAD NEWS TO US GENTLY, KARYN?
NOT AT ALL, SENATOR.
I WON'T PRETEND DYSON'S DEATH ISN'T A SET BACK. AND WE LOST A GREAT DEAL OF VALUABLE DATA AND RESOURCES WHEN CYBERDYNE WAS RAZED.
IT'S THE CIRCUMSTANCES OF LAST NIGHT'S EVENTS THAT ARE PARTICULARLY INTERESTING, SIR.
WE RECOVERED A GRADE TWO LIMB SEGMENT FROM THE MILL. THERE SEEMS TO BE NO DOUBT THAT IT WAS TORN FROM A FUNCTIONING UNIT.
ARE YOU SAYING YOU'VE GOT A LIVE ONE AT LAST?
IT'S TOO EARLY TO TELL, MA'AM. WE'RE STILL SWEEPING THE AREA.
BUT I'M SURE YOU CAN SEE THE IMPLICATIONS--
NOT ENTIRELY, Ms. STERN. IT SEEMS TO ME THAT YOU'VE LOST MORE THAN YOU'VE GAINED. PERHAPS IT'S TIME TO REVIEW YOUR FUNDING AND--
WORST CASE, DYSON'S DEATH WILL SIMPLY SLOW THINGS DOWN A LITTLE. I'M FULLY CONFIDENT I CAN PICK UP WHERE HE LEFT OFF.
I HAVE COMPLETE FAITH IN KARYN'S ABILITY, MA'AM.
WE MIGHT JUST HAVE TO REVISE THE SCHEDULE. NOTHING MORE.

OKAY, BOTTOM LINE. WHAT CAN WE EXPECT TO SEE?
WE HAVE PEOPLE SCOURING DYSON'S HOUSE FOR ANY REMNANTS OF HIS NOTES. Mr. SPASKY IS ALSO DUE TO INTERVIEW DYSON'S WIDOW LATER TODAY.
AND THERE'S ANOTHER ELEMENT. PAGE SEVEN OF YOUR COPIES...
...THIS ONE CAME AT US FROM LEFT FIELD. HER NAME IS SARAH CONNOR. UNTIL YESTERDAY, SHE WAS A PATIENT AT PESCADERO STATE HOSPITAL.
I'VE RESEARCHED HER CASEFILE. SEEMS THAT FOR THE LAST DECADE, SHE HAS BEEN INSISTING THAT BOTH HERSELF AND HER SON HAVE BEEN TARGETS FOR TIME TRAVELLING CYBORGS.
SHE CALLS THEM "TERMINATORS."
IRONIC, ISN'T IT?
YOU'VE NEVER MADE THIS CONNECTION BEFORE?
TWENTY FOUR HOURS AGO, SARAH CONNOR WAS A PITIABLE, PARANOID FRUITCAKE.
SHE WAS AT CYBERDYNE AND WILMINGTON LAST NIGHT. SUDDENLY, WE'VE GOT TO TAKE HER SERIOUSLY.
FINDING HER IS OUR TOP PRIORITY.
WE COULD BE ON THE VERGE OF UNLOCKING GREATER SECRETS THAN WE EVER ANTICIPATED.
LADIES AND GENTLEMEN, WE'RE VERY CLOSE. AND, AS LAST NIGHT HAS SHOWN US...
...YOU NEVER KNOW WHAT MIGHT SHOW UP NEXT.

I WAS THINKING.
THINKING WHAT?
QUICK SHOP
JOHN?
I MEAN... IF WE WON WHEN WE *SLAGGED* THAT THING, WHY DIDN'T THE OTHER TERMINATOR DISAPPEAR?
WHY DIDN'T I DISAPPEAR?
SAY WE'VE *WON*, RIGHT?
WELL, THEN ... WE'VE STOPPED IT ALL FROM HAPPENING. BUT IF WE STOPPED IT FROM HAPPENING, WHY HAS IT *HAPPENED*?
I'M ONLY HERE BECAUSE REESE CAME BACK. HE ONLY CAME BACK BECAUSE THERE WAS *THAT* FUTURE TO COME BACK *FROM*.
THE FUTURE WITH SKYNET, I MEAN.
DOESN'T THAT MEAN THAT SKYNET IS GONNA HAPPEN *WHATEVER* WE DO?
I DON'T KNOW. REESE NEVER HAD TIME TO BRIEF ME ON THE CAUSE-AND-EFFECT OF TIME TRAVEL. I DON'T THINK *HE* REALLY UNDERSTOOD HIMSELF.
"ONE POSSIBLE FUTURE" HE CALLED IT. LIKE THESE WERE *ALTERNATE* ROUTES WE COULD TAKE...
MAX
... I GUESS IF THE FUTURE *ISN'T* SET, THEN THERE MUST BE ONE VERSION WHERE SKYNET *WILL* EXIST.
AND ONE WHERE WE *HAVE* WON.
LET'S HOPE THAT'S THE ONE *WE'RE* LIVING IN, HUH?

...CAN'T YOU JUST LEAVE IT?
WHA' S'MATTER, YOU GOT A HOT DATE?
DINER
MAYBE I HAVE.
YEAH, RIGHT.
GOT NOTHING ON THAT JERK SPASKY. BUT THE BEEMER WAS REGISTERED TO A KARYN STERN...
THE BABE.
RIGHT, SHAKESPEARE. THE BABE.
SHE WORKS OUT OF A PLACE CALLED "NETWORK DEVELOPMENTS" IN SIMI VALLEY. BIG "N", BIG "W", IF YOU PLEASE.
PASS THE SWEET 'N' LOW.
I GET YOU NOW! A DOLL LIKE THAT, A LOWLIFE COP LIKE YOU... HEY, IT COULD WORK!
WILL YOU GIVE ME A BREAK! I'M BEING SERIOUS HERE!
REAL SERIOUS. I KNOW WHAT I SAW TODAY. I KNOW THE FUSS THE FEDS WERE MAKING TO HUSH IT UP. AND I KNOW WHAT I'M THINKING.
AND IT SCARES ME, MAN. IT REALLY SCARES ME.
THAT CONNOR WOMAN MIGHT'VE BEEN TELLING THE TRUTH...

ROUTE 99--
NEAR
BAKERSFIELD.

♪ ...STILL STANDING,
BETTER THAN I EVER DID,
LOOKING LIKE A TRUE
SURVIVOR,
FEELING LIKE A
LITTLE KID... ♪

♪ ...STILL STANDING,
AFTER ALL THIS TIME,
PICKING UP THE
PIECES OF MY LIFE
WITHOUT YOU
ON MY M— ♪

SKZCZZZCH

SKZZZCH

SKKZZKK

COME ON, YOU SUMBISH...

FMMP

SKREEE
SKIIIK
SKREE
WHAT THE HELL HAPPENED?
GEEZ, MAN. I DUNNO.
LOOKED LIKE LIGHTNING HIT THE BLACK-TOP...
DID YOU SAY LIGHTNING?
YEAH. EVERYONE OKAY BACK THERE?
YEAH, YEAH...DID YOU SAY LIGHTNING?
HOLY MOTHER OF MERCY.
OH, MY.

NEXT ISSUE:

"IT CAME LOOKING FOR HER, YOU SEE. AND GOD HELP ANYTHING OR ANYONE THAT STOOD IN ITS WAY.
"WEST HIGHLAND POLICE STATION, BACK IN '84. THAT WAS THE FIRST TIME. SEVENTEEN COPS DEAD, BUT YOU KNOW THAT.
HOMIC
TERMINATOR 2: JUDGMENT DAY
SEARCH MODE
Dan Abnett • writer
Rod Whigham & Gordon Purcell • pencillers
Jack Snider & Inker X • inkers
Patrick Owsley • letterer
Malibu Color • interior color
Mark Paniccia • line editor
Tom Roberts • color design
Dan Shaheen • editor
Rob Prior • cover art
• story by Dan Abnett & Mark Paniccia
"SEVENTEEN DEAD. SEVENTEEN. SEVENTEEN.
"AND THEN LAST NIGHT, A DECADE LATER... IT CAME LOOKING AGAIN."

OKAY.
WHAT ELSE CAN YOU TELL US ABOUT SARAH CONNOR, DOCTOR SILBERMAN?
WELL, IT'S ALL IN MY NOTES, DETECTIVE. THOUGH THEY'LL HAVE TO BE SERIOUSLY REVISED NOW, OF COURSE.
SHE'S BEEN IN MY CARE FOR THE LAST 2 YEARS. A VERY... PROBLEM-ATIC CASE.

YOU MEAN SHE WAS CRAZY.

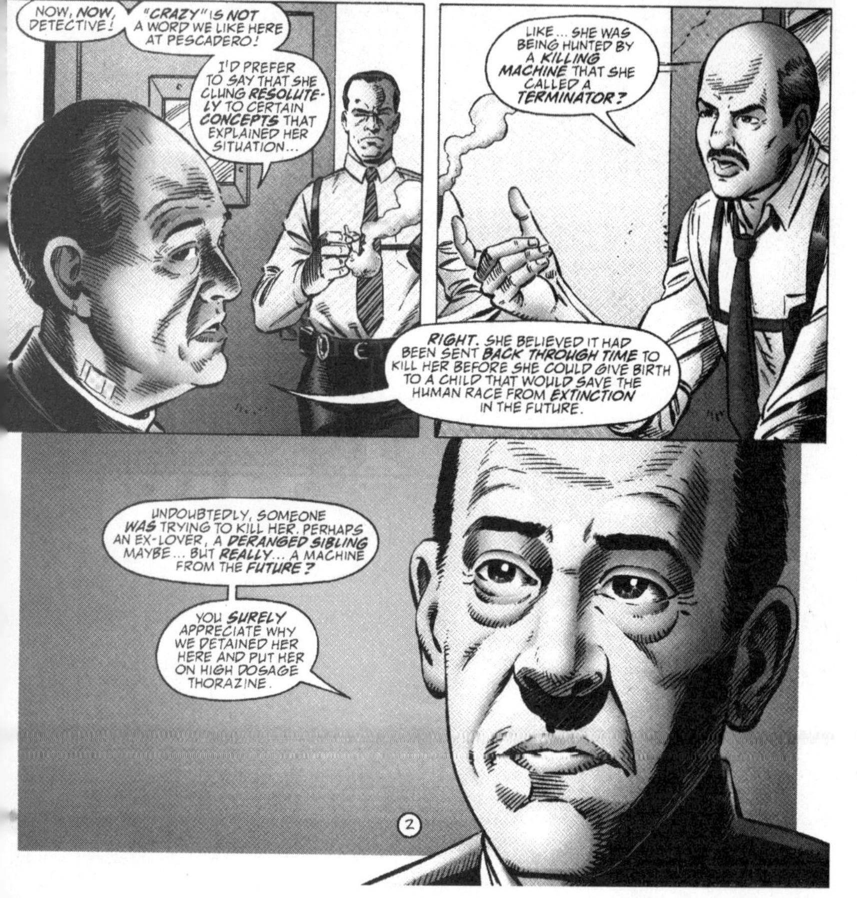
NOW, NOW, DETECTIVE!
"CRAZY" IS NOT A WORD WE LIKE HERE AT PESCADERO!
I'D PREFER TO SAY THAT SHE CLUNG RESOLUTE-LY TO CERTAIN CONCEPTS THAT EXPLAINED HER SITUATION...
LIKE... SHE WAS BEING HUNTED BY A KILLING MACHINE THAT SHE CALLED A TERMINATOR?
RIGHT. SHE BELIEVED IT HAD BEEN SENT BACK THROUGH TIME TO KILL HER BEFORE SHE COULD GIVE BIRTH TO A CHILD THAT WOULD SAVE THE HUMAN RACE FROM EXTINCTION IN THE FUTURE.
UNDOUBTEDLY, SOMEONE WAS TRYING TO KILL HER. PERHAPS AN EX-LOVER, A DERANGED SIBLING MAYBE... BUT REALLY... A MACHINE FROM THE FUTURE?
YOU SURELY APPRECIATE WHY WE DETAINED HER HERE AND PUT HER ON HIGH DOSAGE THORAZINE.

BUT AFTER LAST NIGHT?
WEEELLL... I'M CERTAINLY GOING TO REVIEW MY APPRAISAL OF HER DELUSIONAL ARCHITECTURE.
SO YOU GIVE CREDENCE TO HER STORY NOW?
WELL, NATURALLY!
DO I LOOK LIKE I'M CRAZY?
SO?
SO WHAT?
SO HE'S RAVING? SO THEY'VE GOT HIM ON HAPPY PILLS?
THINK I'D BE WEARING A BUTTON-UP-THE-BACK NUMBER IF I'D BEEN THROUGH WHAT HE WENT THROUGH LAST NIGHT.
I'M GONNA HATE MYSELF FOR ASKING THIS, BUT... YOU BELIEVE HIM, RIGHT?
PESCADERO STATE HOSPIT
STATE OF CALIF
MINALLY DISORDERED
401
I DO.
I DON'T WANT TO...
...BUT I DO.

SOMEWHERE IN L.A....
HEY, HEY... CHECK THAT OUT!

LOOKS LIKE SOMEONE TOOK THE WRONG TURN!
LOOKS THAT WAY TO ME!
WHAT'CHA DOIN' HERE, YOU MOTHERS? YOUR RIDE BROKE DOWN?

I SAID, WHAT'CHA DOING HERE, ASSHOLE?
THIS IS OUR TURF!
THIS-IS-OUR-TURF.
ARE YOU DISSIN' ME, JERK OFF?
BAMM!
BLAMM!
YEEEECHHK!

WASTE 'IM!
BAMM
BLAM
BLAMM
SHOOT 'IM DEAD!

BAMM
BAMM
THUK!
WHUKK!
THKK

UHKK!
AGHH!
HOLY SH-!
YOU ASKED FOR THIS BITCH! YOU ASKED FO--
UHHKK-KK!

USA
USA
SHUNKK!
USA
USA
RRR-CHAKK!

NEARBY...
WELL?
THEY'RE IN THERE, JOHN.
I JUST SAW DYSON'S WIFE AT A WINDOW. THIRD FLOOR.
DELIVERY
WE ARE GONNA GET SO BUSTED, TAILING FEDS ACROSS TOWN.
I'D BET REAL MONEY THEY SAW US WATCHING DYSON'S PLACE.
COME ON. YOU KNOW I'M BETTER THAN THAT.
THE FEDS HAD TO'VE MOVED THEM TO A SAFE HOUSE. STAKING THEIR HOME AND THEN FOLLOWING THE SUITS WAS OUR ONLY WAY OF FINDING THEM.
BUT YOU'RE RIGHT.
THE PLACE IS CRAWLING WITH GOVERNMENT PERSONNEL.
WE'RE GOING TO HAVE TO WAIT FOR AN OPENING.

PLEASE, MRS. DYSON... TARISSA...
DON'T CALL ME THAT, YOU EVIL SON OF A BITCH!
MOMMY? MOMMY? DON'T, MOMMY...
YOU'VE NO RIGHT! YOU'VE NO RIGHT!
I'M SORRY! I'M SORRY, MRS. DYSON...
I CAN APPRECIATE THIS IS A DIFFICULT TIME FOR YOU, BUT WE HAVE TO RUN THROUGH THIS AGAIN...
WE DON'T HAVE TO RUN THROUGH ANYTHING, AGENT SPASKY! WE DON'T HAVE TO DO ANY DAMN THING WE DON'T WANT TO!
MY KIDS ARE SCARED. THEY WANT THEIR DADDY. AND HE'S NOT COMING BACK!
...MILES ISN'T COMING BACK...
EASY NOW, TARISSA...
MOM? DON'T CRY.
MOMMY?

DON'T YOU COME ON WITH THAT! DON'T YOU DARE!
SWAK!
OWK!
GET OUT AND STAY OUT, MISTER.
HUMMH.
OKAY, MRS. DYSON. WE'LL DO THIS LATER.
YOU'RE UPSET. I CAN UNDERSTAND THAT.

SLAM
IT'S OKAY... IT'S OKAY...
...I'M GONNA GET YOU OUT OF HERE...

STEEL MILL-- WILMINGTON...
...SPECIAL AGENT STERN, FBI.
YOU'RE CLEAR TO PROCEED, MS. STERN.
POLICE LINE DO NOT CROSS POLICE L
KLIK
KARYN STERN, SPECIAL OPERATIONS EXECUTIVE, SIMI VALLEY PROJECT. IT'S TWENTY TWO HUNDRED AND I'VE JUST RETURNED TO THE WILMINGTON SITE FOR A FINAL CHECK.
WHILE WE AWAIT AGENT SPASKY'S REPORT ON THE DYSONS AND THE LAB SPECS ON THE RECOVERED EVIDENCE, I HAVE DECIDED TO INSPECT THE MILL ONCE MORE BEFORE IT IS CLEARED AND RE-OPENED.

THE GRADE TWO LIMB SEGMENT WAS RECOVERED FROM THE MILL ASSEMBLY HERE, AT POINT ALPHA BRAVO ON THE SCHEMATICS.
NOTE THAT THE MILL OWNERS ARE TO BE REIMBURSED FOR THE DISMANTLING COSTS.

I... I CAN ALMOST *FEEL* IT HERE, TRAPPED, CRUSHED, TRYING TO GET FREE.
I WONDER IF IT FELT *PAIN* AS IT TORE ITSELF LOOSE?

STRIKE THAT! OF *COURSE* IT DIDN'T!
I'VE STUDIED THIS STUFF LONG ENOUGH TO KNOW THAT THE SENSORY RELAYS ARE PROBABLY *SIGNIFICANTLY INFERIOR* TO HUMAN NEURAL SYSTEMS.

WE'VE SAMPLE-TESTED ALL AROUND THE SITE. PERHAPS SOMETHING ELSE WILL TURN UP.
AN INITIAL SCLEROGRAPHIC ASSAY HAS SHOWN UNUSUAL ALLOYS IN THIS SMELTING VAT... THAT'S POINT ALPHA LIMA ON THE PLANS.
DO NOT CROSS
LEFT OF POINT ALPHA LIMA IS--
ODD. THERE SEEMS TO BE A '94 PONTIAC ON THE LOADING DOCK. CALIFORNIA PLATES. I DON'T REMEMBER THAT BEING THERE BEFORE...
IT'S MINE.
WHO THE--
NO! Oh NO!
SH-CHUK!
THAT WAS QUICK.
NOT CROSS
THERE WAS NOTHING TO SEE.

The hotel stays tight till dawn. We sleep in the car.
I'm starting to have second thoughts about this. I want to see the Dysons again. I need to. But I can't risk exposure to the authorities.
Maybe we should cut our losses here. It's a long drive to the mountains.
mmmnnnhh
W'TIME'SIT?
EARLY.
WHERE ARE YOU GOING?
STRETCH MY LEGS. SCOPE AROUND.
DON'T SWEAT IT, MOM.
I want to stop him, but I know I shouldn't.
John's life is his own, no matter what. If I suffocate him with protection, I'll be doing him no favors in the days that might come.
And I won't be here to watch over him forever.
He's got to make his own choices. He's got to make his own future.

WELCOME
WELCOME
LONG NIGHT eh, SUCKER?
"Check this. Sleeping Beauty" he mouths at me.
GIVE ME STRENGTH...
STAIRS
HELLO? WAKE UP CALL...
YEEECK
Huh?

STAIRS
HEY!
Oh MY GOD! YOU!
DING!
THERE! THERE THEY ARE, FOR GOD'S SAKE!
Oh MAN!
What's he doing in there? What's taking so long?
STOP! HOLD IT THERE! YOU HEAR ME, LADY?
COME ON! IT'S CHECK OUT TIME!
Oh GOD! Oh GOD!
MOMMY? MOMMY?
COME

STOP THEM!
WHAT THE HECK--?
HOLY--!
FRUNCHHH!
WHOA! BRUTAL!
SCREEEEEEE-KKK!
HEY...
...LIBERTYVILLE?
GET IN!
CONNOR! IT'S CONNOR!

I DO NOT BELIEVE THIS! WHAT ARE YOU? TRANQUILIZED?
...COULDA KILLED ME...
SHE SHOULDA, YOU WASTE OF SPACE! GET OUT OF THE WAY!
SPASKY TO OPERATIONS! WE HAVE THREE ABSCONDING WITNESSES SOUTHBOUND ON WESTERN! BACK UP REQUESTED!
ROGER, AGENT SPASKY. AM SHOWING YOU IN PURSUIT.
PUT THE CALL OUT ON THE POLICE BAND! WE'LL NEED ASSIST CUTTING THEM OFF!
ADVISE ALL ELEMENTS THAT SARAH CONNOR IS WITH THE ABSCONDEES. POST HER AS DANGEROUS AND ARMED.
I... JUST WANTED TO GET OUT OF THERE. I COULDN'T STAND THEIR QUESTIONS ANYMORE.
I CAN'T BELIEVE YOU WERE JUST THERE LIKE THAT...
HEY, TIMING IS OUR SPECIALTY.
THEY'RE ON US. CLOSING.
YEAH.
DRAG.
Oh LORD. WHAT WILL THEY DO WITH US WHEN THEY CATCH US?
THEY WON'T CATCH US.

THANKS.
HAVE A NICE ONE.

HEY, MAN. YOUR BUDDY WANTS YOU.
WHAT?
MOSSBERG! MOSSBERG! GET YOUR BUTT OVER HERE!

LITTLE
WHAT'S GOING ON?
GET IN! IT JUST CAME OVER THE AIR!

WHAT DID?
CONNOR!
POSITIVE MAKE AND ONLY EIGHT BLOCKS AWAY. THEY'RE CALLING DOWN EVERYTHING ON HER, BUT WE'RE CLOSE.
...REPEAT, ALL UNITS. SUSPECT SOUTHBOUND ON WESTERN. '90 GREEN NISSAN PATHFINDER. ASSISTANCE REQUESTED...

...SUSPECT SARAH CONNOR, WANTED IN CONNECTION WITH A CODE 999 AT IRVINE THURSDAY. SUSPECT REPORTED AS ARMED AND DANGEROUS. PROCEED WITH CAUTION...
REALISTIC

...REPEAT, ALL UNITS. SUSPECT SOUTHBOUND ON WESTERN...

HOLD ON.
Oh MY GOD!

Oh F--

WHUUNNNGHH

TOO FAST!
DID YA SEE?
CRAZY MAN
DAMN! DAMN! DAMN!
WHAT'S YOUR GAME, ASSHOLE?

WHCHK!
EHGG!
GET OUT OF MY LIFE, PINHEAD.
SPASKY TO OPERATIONS. I'M OUT OF THE CHASE! FOR GOD'S SAKE, GET THE LOCAL GEEKS TO CUT HER OFF AT WASHINGTON BEFORE SHE MAKES THE INTERSTATE.
UNDERSTOOD...

WEEOOOEEOOO
AW NUTS! NOW WE GOT COPS!
WEEOOOEEOOO
EEEOOOEEOO
I SEE THEM, JOHN.
ARE YOU STRAPPED IN?
Oh PLEASE!
REALITY CHECK, MOTHER. "FATE OF THE WORLD?" "ROAD SAFETY?" WHAT'S WRONG WITH THIS PICTURE?
EVERYTHING. TRUST ME.
THUMP
AAAAIIGH!
SHOOT!
EEEERRRRK
POLICE

BACK! BACK IT UP!
WAY COOL...
...WAY, WAY COOL.
YOU LIKED THAT, huh?
...GONNA KILL US ALL. YOU'RE GONNA KILL US ALL...
...YOU KILLED MILES AND NOW YOU'RE GONNA--
Oh MY GOD! Oh MY GOD! AHEAD OF US! AHEAD OF US!
MOM!
DAMN!
SARAH! SARAH CONNOR!
SKREEEEEEEEEEE!
WEATHERBY, L.A.P.D.! DON'T DO ANYTHING CRAZY, SARAH! I WANT TO HELP YOU!
Trapped. Cruisers closing behind, plain clothes in front.
I was enjoying this too much. I was stupid.
And we're all going to pay the price.
Unless...

OUT OF THE WAY! NOW!
DON'T DO THIS, SARAH! I WANT TO HELP! PLEASE!
MOM! NO! THEY'RE JUST COPS!
I SAID BACK!
DON'T YOU REMEMBER ME, SARAH? I CAME TO SEE YOU AT PESCADERO! ABOUT THE TERMINATORS!
SHLKK
ENOUGH, MAN! LEAVE IT!
I BELIEVE, SARAH! I BELIEVE THEY EXIST! I WANT TO HELP YOU!
TRUST ME! I'LL CALL THE UNIFORMS OFF! I'LL GET IMMUNITY FOR YOU!
I'VE HEARD THAT TOO MANY TIMES BEFORE!
DON'T MAKE ME HURT YOU, WEATHERBY.
PLEASE, SARAH...
WHAT CAN I DO TO MAKE YOU BELIEVE ME?
BOOM BOOM BOOM
BUHHKK--!

He falls. He dies. And before I even see why, I know why.
GOD HELP ME...
It wasn't over.
We didn't win.
It's back.
FOOM
FOOM
SARAH CONNOR ...
BABOOOOM!
NISSAN
NEXT:
JUDGMENT IMPAIRED

It's back.
I hoped. I prayed. I fought. But it's back.
Third time's a charm.
Dan Abnett writer •
Rod Whigham penciller •
Jack Snider inker •
Patrick Owsley letterer •
Shannon Blanchard color design •
Malibu Color interior color •
Dan Shaheen editor •
Rod Whigham & Chuck Maiden cover art •
story by Dan Abnett Mark Paniccia & Gerry Kline
JUDGMENT IMPAIRED
TERMINATOR® 2: JUDGMENT DAY

JOHN! JOHN! GET DOWN! STAY DOWN!
Weatherby. Did he mean it when he said he believed me?
Moot point, now walking proof has shot him dead.
I try to catch his partner's eye...
...no joy. All he can see is his friend's butchered corpse.
BRAAAKKK
It's out of ammo.
Three seconds to reload, tops.
chkk-!
chkk!

Make them count.
BLAMM
BAMM
BLAMM
BAMM
But they don't. They never do. There's never enough time.
SHLAKK
WHAT?!
CHKK!
WHHUMMCH
SKREEEEEEEE

CONNOR! COME ON! COME ON, DAMMIT!
MOM?
GO! GO! GO! MOVE IT!
Oh MY GOD! Oh MY GOD!
DRIVE! DRIVE!
SHREEEEEEEEE
...REPEAT! OFFICER DOWN! MULTIPLE GUNSH--
Oh MY GOD! CHECK THIS OUT!

SCANNING
9004 46
5774 00
2554 61
5721 44
4571 99
0034 76
04992
48299
59285
28850
27499
00371
SEARCH MODE
STOP! POLICE!
BAM
BAM BAM
DROP IT! DROP IT NOW!
BIKK
AGHH!
AYKK!
SHHREEEEEE

WHAT'S YOUR NAME?
MOSSBERG.
THAT WAS FAST THINKING BACK THERE, MOSSBERG, BUT WE'LL HAVE TO DO MORE IF WE'RE GOING TO STAY ALIVE.
THAT WAS... ONE OF THOSE THINGS, WASN'T IT? LIKE WEATHERBY SAID.
RIGHT.
OH JESUS.
KEEP IT TOGETHER! IT'S IN THE CRUISER BEHIND US AND IT'S CLOSING.
I NEED YOU SHARP, MOSSBERG!
MOM!
BFFUMCHH
AHHH!
B-LAM!

THERE! THERE! THE CONSTRUCTION SITE!
EVANS CONSTRUCTION
OKAY!
WHHUNNCHHKK!
COME ON! STAY TOGETHER! THROUGH TO THE LEFT!
WE'RE DEAD!
NO ONE DIES TILL I TELL THEM THEY CAN!
7

SIMI VALLEY, CALIFORNIA.
EARLY START TODAY, MS. STERN?
NetWork DEVELOPMENTS
THAT'S RIGHT.
HAVE A NICE ONE.
THANKS. YOU TOO.
NW SECURITY
KARYN STERN SPEAKING.
KARYN! IT'S SPASKY! GET A LOAD OF THIS!
IT'S CONNOR! SHE SPRUNG THE DYSONS FROM THE SAFE HOUSE LOCATION!
WHERE ARE YOU?
IN PURSUIT! BUT THERE'S MORE! I THINK WE HAVE A FUNCTIONING UNIT DOWN HERE AFTER THEM!
SOMETHING TOOK THE COPS APART TO GET AT CONNOR! I MEAN, IT, KARYN! A LIVE ONE! I'VE GOT SPE-CIAL OPS COMING IN TO BACK ME UP!
DID YOU HEAR ME, KARYN? A LIVE ONE!
I HEARD YOU.
KEEP ME INFORMED.
8

'BUD'
THWMMFMP!
One thing I've learned through all of this.
You can only run so far.
Running just gets you tired and delays the inevitable.
The only way to live is to turn and fight.
RASH
9

OVER HERE, YOU SON OF A BITCH!
BAMM! BAMM! BLAMM!
BOOOM! BOOOM!
GAAAH!
THUNNK! CHOON
RACHIKK!
HAIL MARY, FULL OF GRACE ...
OH
GOD
HELP

BRRMMMFFF!
BRRRMMMFM-MCHH!
WHMMCH!
KLNNG-GGNNCH!
COME ON!
COME ON!

NOOO!

KRUNTCHHH!

Y-YOU KILLED IT.
WASN'T EVER ALIVE.
STAY BACK. THE POWER CORE IS HOUSED IN THE CHEST, SO IT'S PROBABLY SCRAGGED, BUT YOU CAN'T TAKE A CHANCE WITH THESE BASTARDS.
SO LET'S GO! GET OUT OF HERE!
WE CAN'T LEAVE IT HERE.
WHAT? LIKE HELL WE CAN'T!
JOHN'S RIGHT.
I'M ALWAYS RIGHT...
IF WE DITCH IT AND IT ISN'T DEAD, WE'LL HAVE SUCKERED OURSELVES.
AND AFTER THE TROUBLE WE WENT THROUGH AT CYBERDYNE, WE CAN'T LEAVE IT HERE TO BE FOUND.
BUT IT MUST WEIGH HALF A TON...!
THEN WE TAKE WHAT REALLY MATTERS...

CAREFUL!
DON'T HAVE A COW, MOM. JUST WATCH THE EYES. IF YOU SEE RED...
...JOHN'S DEAD.
YES! AND THE CROWD GOES WILD!
CHAKK
AND FOR MY NEXT TRICK!
THAT'S ENOUGH, JOHN.
KEEP IT SAFE. NOW LET'S MOVE.
WHERE D'YOU LEARN TO DO THAT?
MY UNCLE SHOWED ME HOW.
The terminator's CPU was the one thing we couldn't let the authorities have.
Working with only a damaged version, Miles Dyson had all but constructed the basis of Skynet. And then he gave his life to stop that from happening.
But everything we won that night at Cyberdyne seems to have been lost again. This terminator is proof that the Skynet future is still fact.
Despite the immediate threat of the sirens yowling in the streets outside, hunting for us, I need to know why.

INSIDE NETWORK DEVELOPMENTS...
YOU'LL HURT YOUR EYES, KARYN.
WHAT?
YOU'RE SCROLLING THE SCREEN SO FAST, YOU'LL HURT YOUR EYES.
YOU CAN'T BE TAKING ANYTHING IN.
NO, OF COURSE NOT.
I'M JUST... THINKING.
KARYN! I'VE GOT SPASKY ON LINE FIVE!
PICK UP QUICK! HE SOUNDS LIKE HE'S GONNA HAVE A CORONARY!
SPASKY?
KARYN! I'M WITH SPECIAL OPS AT A CONSTRUCTION SITE OFF FAIRFAX!
WE'VE GOT ONE!
15

IT'S TAKEN A POUNDING, BUT EVERTHING SEEMS TO BE HERE! IT'S STILL GOT PARTS OF THE SYNTHETIC FLESH ATTACHED!
RETRIEVAL IS BAGGING IT UP RIGHT NOW! GET AN INSPECTION SUITE READY TO RECEIVE!
KARYN, THIS IS *INCREDIBLE*!
THE COPS ARE GOING MAD BECAUSE I WON'T LET THEM INTO THE SCENE! CAN YOU GET ON THE HORN TO CITY HALL AND PULL RANK?
OF COURSE.
EXPECT US IN TWO HOURS.
GOOD NEWS?
UM, YES. GOOD NEWS.

We go to ground in a motel on the interstate.
Running any further in daylight would leave us wide open to the authorities.
Now we have a chance to piece things together.
... THE FEDS WERE ALL OVER THE MILL. WEATHERBY GOT INSIDE. HE SAW... AN ARM, WEDGED IN SOME GEARS.
THAT WAS WHAT... CONVINCED HIM.
THERE'S GOT TO BE MORE TO IT.
WHAT DO YOU MEAN "MORE"?
THEY COULD LEARN A LOT FROM THE ARM... MECHANICAL SYSTEMS, ALLOYS, PERIPHERAL ELECTRONICS.
BUT NOTHING ABOUT THE MACHINE'S BRAIN. NOTHING THAT COULD LEAD THEM TO SKYNET. SOMETHING ELSE MUST GIVE THEM THE EDGE...
A-ARE YOU SAYING MILES DIED FOR NOTHING?
IS THAT WHAT YOU'RE SAYING?!?
EASY! TAKE IT EASY!
C'MON, LADY, PLEASE.

HOW MUCH DO YOU UNDERSTAND OF THIS, MOSSBERG?
NOT A WHOLE HELL OF A LOT.
THESE ARE ROBOTS. RIGHT? KILLER ROBOTS FROM THE FUTURE?
POSSIBLE FUTURE, BADGE. GET IT RIGHT.
THERE'S A FUTURE OUT THERE RULED BY A GRIEVOUS COMPUTER CALLED SKYNET. A COMPUTER WE CREATE.
IT'S TOTALLY BAD NEWS FOR EVERYONE.
THIS IS WHAT WE KNOW, MOSSBERG-- IN AUGUST 1997, STRATEGIC DEFENSE DECISIONS ARE HANDED OVER TO A MILITARY COMPUTER SYSTEM CALLED SKYNET.
WITHIN WEEKS, IT BECOMES SELF-AWARE, AND OBLITERATES HUMANITY AS A LOGICAL EXTENSION OF ITS PROGRAMMED WILL TO PROTECT ITSELF.
FROM THE ASHES OF GENOCIDE, HUMANITY FIGHTS BACK. EVENTUALLY, HUMANITY WINS, THANKS TO THE LEADERSHIP OF ONE, INSPIRED LEADER.
MY SON, JOHN CONNOR.
HEY, NO AUTOGRAPHS.
THAT'S WHY THE TERMINATORS WERE SENT BACK. TO KILL HIM. TO MAKE SURE HE NEVER EXISTS.
TO MAKE SURE SKYNET WON'T LOSE.
18

BUT THAT WAS WHY YOU CAME AFTER MILES! TO STOP THIS SKYNET FROM HAPPENING!
YOU SAID HE WAS RESPON-SIBLE!
HE WAS! HE WAS! AND WE CHANGED THAT!
BUT IT WASN'T ENOUGH! NOW THERE'S SOMETHING ELSE...SOME OTHER FACTOR THAT MEANS SKYNET WILL STILL COME TO BE!
BUT WE DESTROYED EVERYTHING. ALL HIS NOTES, ALL HIS FILES...
...AND HE'S DEAD.
THE GOVERNMENT AGENTS QUESTIONED ME FOR SO LONG. THEY WERE DESPERATE. THEY CAN'T HAVE HAD ANY-THING LEFT.
THEN WE MUST HAVE MISSED SOMETHING.
OR SOMETHING NEW HAS ENTERED THE PICTURE. AND I DON'T KNOW WHERE TO START SEARCH-ING FOR IT.
THERE'S A PLACE IN SIMI VALLEY. NETWORK DEVELOPMENTS. WEATHERBY TRACKED IT DOWN. THE FEDS WE WERE WATCHING WORKED OUT OF THERE.

THEN THAT'S WHERE I'LL LOOK FIRST.
WHAT'S YOUR NAME, MOSSBERG?
YOU SAID IT, CONNOR. MOSSBERG.
NO, I MEANT ...
DAVID. DAVE.
DAVE... THERE'S A PLACE IN THE MOUNTAINS. JOHN KNOWS IT.
I WANT YOU TO TAKE JOHN AND THE DYSONS THERE AND WAIT FOR ME.
I CAN TELL YOU WHERE TO PICK UP SUPPLIES AND WEAPONS EN ROUTE. YOU MIGHT NEED THEM.
SURE.
I'LL LOOK AFTER THEM, SARAH.
OH, NO WAY! NO WAY, MOM!
YES WAY, JOHN! YOU KNOW THE SCORE!
SO DO I.
DANNY AND BLYTHE CAN GO WITH THE COP, BUT I'M COMING WITH YOU.
20

THE SKULL SOCKET'S EMPTY.
YOU CHECKED THE AREA CAREFULLY?
YEAH, NO SIGN.
CONNOR MUST'VE STRIPPED IT OUT AND TAKEN IT. SHE KNOWS HER STUFF.
I'VE GOT ALL AVAILABLE PERSONNEL SEARCHING FOR HER.
LET'S HOPE THEY FIND HER.
SURE.
SHALL I TAKE THIS BABY DOWN TO R&D AND TURN THE BOYS LOOSE ON IT?
YOU DO THAT.
OKAY, LET'S GO!
DEEB
DIP
DEEB DIP

BREEP
BREEP

BREEP
BREE-KLK!
YES?
TRUCK STOP
IGGY
LOS
LAURA
NEXT: GENESIS AND REVELATIONS

EXCUSE ME...
...MY NAME IS SARAH CONNOR.
AND I'D LIKE TO SEE WHOEVER'S IN CHARGE HERE.
Dan Abnett • writer
Rod Whigham & Jack Snider • art
Patrick Owsley letterer •
Moose Baumann interior color • & design
Dan Shaheen editor •
Rod Whigham & Chuck Maiden cover art •
Story by Dan Abnett & Mark Paniccia
GENESIS & REVELATIONS
TERMINATOR® 2: JUDGMENT DAY
PUSH
STU
MUFFI
1 2 3

uh
ah
erm
SURELY. JUST A MOMENT.
NEDERMEYER
NETWORK DEVELOPMENTS, SIMI VALLEY, CA.
FINE.
UH... THIS IS RECEPTION. I HAVE A-- UH-- SARAH CONNOR HERE, WISHING TO SPEAK WITH... WITH SOMEONE IN CHARGE.
YES.
THAT IS CORRECT.
FINE. I'LL DO THAT.
SOMEONE WILL BE DOWN RIGHT AWAY.
THANK YOU.
PLEASE-- UH-- TAKE A SEAT.
WE DON'T HAVE TO GO THAT FAR.

FREEZE! NOT A TWITCH, CONNOR! NOT ONE MOVE!
GET DOWN ON THE FLOOR WITH YOUR HANDS BEHIND YOUR HEAD! NOW!
FAN OUT! SURROUND HER!
oh JESUS!
YOU'RE SPASKY, RIGHT?
YOU'RE THE ONE I WANTED TO SEE.
I CAN TELL YOU NOW, I'M UNARMED.
LOTTI

SHE'S CLEAN.
I TOLD YOU.
SHUT UP!
THIS IS SOME KIND OF TRICK! THE BITCH IS FULL OF DAMN TRICKS!
YOU'VE GOT A NINE TO THE BACK OF MY SKULL, SPASKY.
IF THIS IS A TRICK, IT'S NOT A VERY GOOD ONE, IS IT?
SHE HAS A POINT, SPASKY.
HAVE YOU THOUGHT OF ASKING HER WHAT SHE WANTS?
NO...
WELL, WHY DON'T WE TRY, THEN?
MS. CONNOR? YOUR BUSINESS HERE?
I CAME HERE...
...TO TALK.

HIGHWAY 78, SKIRTING THE CHOCOLATE MOUNTAINS...
THAT EVERYTHING?
POP'S
GIMME SIXTY FILTERLESS. AND I'LL TAKE A COUPLA THESE COMIC BOOKS.
TRAVEL-LING WITH KIDS, huh?
THE COMICS GAVE IT AWAY, RIGHT?
KISS ME I'M IRISH
GUM
NOPE. THE NICOTINE INTAKE.
YOU GOT FAR TO GO?
YEAH, WE--
--WE GOT A... A LONG WAY TO RIDE YET.
HEY NOW, I AIN'T PRYING NONE, YOUNG FELLA!
I WAS JUST MAKING CONVERSATION IS ALL.
SURE, SURE. I'M SORRY.
LOOK, I'LL GET SOME OF THOSE MAR-KER PENS TOO. YOU GOT ANY SKETCH PADS? KIDS LIKE TO DRAW, RIGHT?
MARKERS

WHAT'S THAT STUFF HE'S BUYING?
AH-DUH? WHAT DOES HE WANT PENS FOR?
THAT GUY IS SUCH A LOSER.
HE'S OKAY.
HE'S A PRIZE-WINNING WAD, BLYTHE. AND A BADGE TO BOOT.
I CAN'T BELIEVE MOM SADDLED ME WITH HIM.
US.
Huh?
SADDLED US. ALL OF US. YOU, ME AND DANNY. WE'RE A TEAM, MR MOSSBERG SAID.
DID HE? Pheeeww! WHAT IS HE ON?
HEY, DANNY! WHA'CHA DOING?
DOING?
N-NUTHIN'.
YOU BETTER NOT HAVE WHAT I THINK YOU GOT, SHRIMP!.
I AIN'T GOT NUTHIN', JOHN! I SWEAR!
GIVE ME THE C.P.U., DANNY.
YOU HEAR ME, DYSON? GIVE!
GIVE IT TO ME AND I WON'T TELL MOSSBERG YOU WERE FOOLIN' WITH IT, OKAY?

SORR-REE!
I JUST WANTED TO LOOK AT IT...
LEMME SEE IT!
NO!
OKAY, OKAY... I'M SORRY I YELLED. NO HARM DONE.
JUST REMEMBER... THIS THING IS A... A... TERMINATOR'S BRAIN. IT'S THE MOST DANGEROUS THING THERE IS. IF IT GETS LOOSE... THEN THERE'S NO SUCH THING AS A FUTURE FOR ANY OF US.
FOR CHRISSAKES, YOUR DAD DIED KEEPING THIS STUFF SECRET!
DON'T CRY, BLYTHE.
I'M NOT.
WE KNOW.
THAT'S WHY WE'RE HERE.
OKAY, POINT.
TRUCE, YEAH? WHADDYA SAY, CHAMP? HERE COMES MOSSBERG.
SURE. TRUCE.
YOU OKAY BACK THERE? I GOT YOU STUFF... CANDY, COMIC BOOKS, PENS...
THANK GOD! HE GOT US PENS!
WHADDYA KNOW... I DID SOMETHING RIGHT.

NETWORK DEVELOPMENTS...
INTERVIEW COMMENCES. IT'S EIGHT MINUTES AFTER TEN, FRIDAY THE FIFTH. INTERVIEW SUBJECT SARAH CONNOR HAS SIGNED A RELEASE STATING SHE IS HERE VOLUNTARILY. PRESENT ARE FEDERAL AGENTS KARYN STERN AND VINCENT SPASKY.
SARAH? PERHAPS YOU'D LIKE TO START.
Make or break time. I've come so far, fought so hard, and now it all depends on words.
Here, in the Lion's Den, my toughest fight. If I'm guessing right, there's stuff going on in this building that will somehow ensure the creation of SkyNet.
But a wholesale assault, like the one we staged at Cyberdyne just a few nights ago, would be pointless and doomed.
The only way for me to win here is to be open, and hope that I can persuade them.
Like I convinced Dyson.
Spasky is a no-one. I can see that now. He's a doer, not a thinker, and I can't afford to waste my time on him.
But Stern. I don't know what it is.
She frightens me.
WELL, SARAH?
I CAME HERE, UNARMED, TO TALK, BECAUSE I BELIEVE THAT HONEST COMMUNICATION MIGHT STILL SAVE THE DAMN SPECIES.
I NEED TO KNOW WHAT YOU'RE DOING HERE. TELL ME, AND I'LL SHARE WITH YOU EVERYTHING I KNOW.
BELIEVE ME, YOU CAN'T AFFORD TO HOLD ANYTHING BACK.
8

DREAM ON, CONNOR! YOU'RE AN ESCAPEE FROM THE PESCADERO NUT-HATCH WHO'S SHOT AND BOMBED HER WAY THROUGH THIS STATE IN DEFIANCE OF THE LAW!
WE'RE REQUIRED TO TELL YOU PRECISELY SQUAT.
VINCENT'S RIGHT, SARAH. YOU HAVE A HISTORY OF PSYCHOTIC EPISODES AND A VERY VIOLENT TRACK RECORD. CAN YOU GIVE US ANY REASON TO EXCHANGE INFORMATION WITH YOU?
ONE-- WE BOTH KNOW ABOUT THE EXISTENCE OF THE MACHINES CALLED TERMINATORS.
TWO-- WE BOTH KNOW THAT THEY REPRESENT A SCENARIO FAR MORE SIGNIFICANT THAN OUR PETTY BICKERING.
THREE-- IF I DON'T WALK OUT OF HERE BY FOUR O'CLOCK THIS AFTERNOON, A PREPARED STATEMENT COVERING EVERYTHING I KNOW ABOUT TERMINATORS COMPLETE WITH CORROBORATING POLICE RECORDS AND DETAILS OF YOUR COMPLICITY, WILL BE DISSEMINATED TO THE MEDIA BY MAIL, FAX AND INTERNET.
YOU'D NEVER CONTAIN IT ALL. IT WOULD BLOW THIS OPERATION WIDE OPEN.
YOU LITTLE--
SPASKY!
VERY THOROUGH MS. CONNOR, BUT WILL ANYONE BELIEVE THE WORD OF AN ESCAPED MENTAL PATIENT?
GIVEN THE CURRENT STATE OF THE MEDIA, CAN YOU AFFORD TO TAKE THAT CHANCE?
TOUCHÉ SARAH, BUT IT WOULD TAKE AN AWFUL LOT OF ORGANIZATION TO GUARANTEE SUCH COVERAGE.
DON'T YOU THINK I'M CAPABLE?

IT'S NOT THAT--
YOUR CELL-PHONE, PLEASE.
WHAT?
GIVE IT TO HER!
OKAY...
THIS IS CONNOR.
I'M IN POSITION.
I'M HANDING YOU OVER NOW.
WELL?
BUT--!?
GO AHEAD. WHO IS THIS?

TARISSA DYSON.
I HAVE SIXTY-FOUR COMMUNIQUES READY FOR DISPATCH VIA EXPRESS POST, FAX AND INTO THREE THOUSAND SEPARATE WEB-SITES ON THE NET.
THEY WILL BE SENT UNLESS I COUNTERMAND THE AUTHORIZATION BEFORE FOUR PM.
DO YOU UNDERSTAND?
PHONE
PHONE
KEEP L.A. CLEAN
USING THE DYSON WIDOW IS A NICE TOUCH.
THANK YOU.
BY THE WAY, SPASKY...DON'T BOTHER RUSHING OUT TO TRACE THAT NUMBER BY THE RE-CALL ON YOUR MOBILE...
...IT'S A PAYPHONE ON SEPULVEDA. TARISSA'S ALREADY GONE.
SO...
...WHERE DOES THAT LEAVE US?
WE'D BETTER SHOW YOU AROUND THEN, SARAH.
THIS WAY...
I CAN'T BELIEVE Y--
Oh, BE QUIET, SPASKY.
SARAH?

COOL.
YOU THINK?
YEAH. YOU REMEMBERED IT WELL.
Gee. LIKE I'M GONNA FORGET.
YOU OKAY BACK THERE, KIDS? GREAT VIEW Huh?
Y-huh!
"GREAT VIEW"...
He-he hee!
JOHN...?
YEAH?
I WAS THINKING... THIS COMPUTER... SKYNET...
WHAT ABOUT IT?

THAT CPU IS A BRAIN, RIGHT? AND BRAINS CAN BE MESSED UP BY DISEASES AND STUFF, RIGHT?
LIKE A VIRUS?
YEAH. VIRUSES CAN KILL COMPUTERS, CAN'T THEY?
MY DAD TOLD ME.
YEAH. SO WHAT?
SO COULDN'T WE KILL SKYNET THAT WAY?
RIGHT.
I MEAN IT, JOHN. SKYNET'S BASIC SOURCE CODE HAS TO BE IN THAT CPU SOMEWHERE...
...THAT'S ALL WE'D NEED. THAT, AND ABOUT A MILLION HOURS OF PROGRAMMING.
YOU SERIOUS, DYSON-BRAT?
DEADLY.
WE COULD DO IT, Y'KNOW.
I COULD DO IT.
ONE DAY I'LL HOLD YOU TO THAT, CHAMP!
HE-E-EY!

PLAY NICE, YOU TWO! Y'HEAR?
OKAY, BADGE.
AND DON'T CALL ME THAT.
Oh
Oh MAN
WHERE'D THAT BASTARD COME FROM?
WHAT BASTARD?
MOSSBERG? BADGE?
OH, PLEASE DON'T TALK THAT WAY, HONEY! YOUR MOM'LL KILL ME!
WHAT IS IT?
BACK THERE, ON THE HOG. SEE HIM?
YEAH.
BASTARD-- BASTARD-- BASTARD-- BASTARD...
SHUT UP, WILL YA! I TOLD YA! F'R CHRISSAKES, I TOLD YA ONCE!
oh-- uh-- uh-- uh-- uh!
AH, DON'T CRY, HONEY! PLEASE! I DIDN'T MEAN IT!
I MEAN THIS, BADGE...
...FLOOR IT, FOR GOD'S SAKE... DRIVE!

BRRRTTT TTTTTTT

BRATTSH!
GET DOWN!
PCKK!
WHUKK!
OH CHRIST!
HOW DID IT FIND US? HOW DID IT FIND US?!
MOSSBERG!
BRTTTT
MOSSBERG! WHICH BAG IS YOUR PIECE IN?
DANNO? DANNO?
Ohhh! Ohhh!
IT HURTS ...
DANNY'S HIT! DANNY'S HIT!
OH YOU SON OF A BITCH!

WHAMMMCHKK!
YOU DIDN'T HAVE TO SHOOT THE KID!
I GOT HIM! I GOT HIM, RIGHT?
I DUNNO, BADGE! I DIDN'T SEE HIM FALL!
SHRAAKKKK-CHH!
NO!
AIIIEEE!
HOLY S--

EAT THIS, DIRTBAG!
BAM
BLAMM
BLAM
BLAMM
CAN WE SHAKE HIM? CAN WE SHAKE HIM?
UGH!
B-BAAMF!
JESUS... NOOOOO!
WHAMMPCCHHH

MEANWHILE, BACK AT NETWORK...
OH MY GOD.
I TAKE IT YOU WEREN'T EXPECTING THIS?
SO... MANY.
WHERE DID THEY ALL COME FROM?
15
16
WE THOUGHT YOU KNEW, SARAH.
THE SAME PLACE AS THE ONES THAT ALLEGEDLY STALKED YOU.
THE FUTURE.
BUT--

--WHY SO MANY?
GUINEA PIGS IS OUR GUESS. THESE UNITS HAVE BEEN RECOVERED BY THE U.S. GOVERNMENT FROM SITES ALL AROUND THE WORLD. THE FIRST WAS FOUND IN ARGENTINA IN THE MID-SEVENTIES.
IN TWO DECADES, WE'VE FOUND TWENTY-SEVEN OF THEM.
WE THINK THE CHINESE HAVE ANOTHER THREE, AND THE FRENCH MAY ALSO HAVE ONE.
NONE HAVE BEEN FOUND FUNCTIONING. NONE OF THEM SURVIVED THEIR TRIP HERE. IT CLEARLY TOOK THEIR MANUFACTURER A LONG TIME TO GET THE MEANS OF TRANSPORTATION TO WORK.
THEY HAVE BEEN THE SUBJECT OF INTENSIVE RESEARCH FOR YEARS. THE VALUE OF THE DERIVED TECHNOLOGY CANNOT BE MEASURED.
BUT WE'D ALWAYS PRAYED FOR ONE TO SURVIVE THE TRANSIT EXPERIENCE AND ARRIVE INTACT, SO THAT WE COULD EXAMINE ITS FUNCTION, ITS LIFE, ITS BRAIN...
OF COURSE, WE HAD NO IDEA WHERE THEY CAME FROM OR HOW OR WHY... UNTIL YOU CAME ALONG WITH THOSE ANSWERS.
YOU'VE GOT TO STOP. YOU'VE GOT TO STOP THIS RIGHT NOW.
YOU HAVE NO IDEA WHAT YOU'RE DOING! THIS IS WHY WE DESTROYED CYBERDYNE! THIS IS WHY DYSON DIED!
THESE... THINGS AREN'T SOME LUCKY BREAK... A SHORT CUT TO NEXT YEAR'S TECHNOLOGY.
THEY'RE THE HERALDS OF DESTRUCTION! SKYNET WANTS YOU TO LEARN! IT WANTS YOU TO LEARN SO THAT YOU CAN BUILD SKYNET!

OH, I HAVE HAD IT WITH YOU!
YOU'RE SO OUT OF YOUR DEPTH HERE IT'S EMB--
SPASKY!
GO AND COOL OFF FOR A MINUTE.
SCREAMING ISN'T GOING TO GET US ANYWHERE.
SO, SARAH... YOU CONVINCED MILES DYSON HE WAS MAKING A MISTAKE AND GOT HIM TO DESTROY HIS WORK.
AND NOW YOU WANT TO TALK SOME SIMILAR SENSE INTO US.
I HAVE TO STOP YOU. SKYNET MUST NEVER HAPPEN.
SO YOU SAY.
AND YOU'LL LEAK THIS ALL TO THE MEDIA TONIGHT IF WE DON'T ACQUIESCE AND LET YOU WALK FREE?
YOU KNOW DAMN WELL I WI--
--GOD! NO!
22

THEN SARAH CONNOR WILL WALK OUT OF HERE THIS AFTERNOON . . .
NEXT: NO FATE

Reese said... there's no fate but what we make for ourselves.
And that's what they're making here, in a vault in Simi Valley, picking up where Dyson and Cyberdyne left off.
Reverse engineering terminator endoskeletons -- aborted time travelers -- for their secrets...
I tried to stop it. I had to try. And in trying, I found what was directing their insane schemes.
Another polyalloy T-1000.
YUUHNN!
Dan Abnett • writer
Rod Whigham & Jack Snider • art
NO FATE
Patrick Owsley • letterer
Moose Baumann • color design
Malibu Color • interior color
Dan Shaheen • editor
Rod Whigam & Joel Naprstek • cover art
Story by Dan Abnett & Mark Paniccia
TERMINATOR 2: JUDGMENT DAY
If there ever was a real Dr. Karyn Stern, my hopes for success here died with her.
Now it intends to terminate me, to try to assume my identity to get at John and the others.
FRATSHH!
Uhhnn!
The alarms should bring others in here, which could be my only chance.
BREEP
BREEP
EXIT
Unless they're all polyalloy killers.

STERN! WHAT THE H--
OH MY GOD!
SPASKY! SHOOT IT! EMPTY YOUR CLIP INTO IT AND FALL BACK FAST!
STAY BACK! STAY BACK!
BAM!
CHAM! CHAM-CHAM! CHAM!
gak.
WHUNNCHHH!
Spasky always said he wanted to meet a live one.
Achieving his ambition has bought me vital seconds.
HOLD IT, CONNOR!
WHAT THE HELL'S GOING ON UP HERE?
NO TIME!
THUKK!
BOOOOH!
EHKK!
WHMMP!

SARAH?
YOU CAN'T LEAVE.
SCREW YOU!
BAM
BAM
BAM
BRAAAPPP!
THATT
FPANG!
THUKK
WUK
WUK
WUK
Those chrome wounds will heal in seconds. It's almost unkillable.
The only way to stop a T-1000 is to freeze it or melt it... or do anything which breaks down its structure at a base level to stop it from reconfiguring.
WEEEB
WEEE
WEEE
So I need a smart plan. And as many distractions as I can get.

Chem-Analysis Lab. Good start.
GET OUT! MOVE!
Just hope I've got time to improvise somethi--
EXIT
LAB 7
WKK-
RASSHH!
Guhh!
I give it everything I've got... everything at hand... sample beakers, dropper trays, test molds... anything not bolted down!
BRAAKATH!
TISHHH!
STRASH!
FTSHH
And just when the H&K runs out, fate steps in.
One flask out of hundreds. A solvent. The label on the broken bottle says 27B/6.
KTIK TK
It freezes the upper layers of the polyalloy like ice on a pond.
CH!

Maybe it makes the alloy inert. Maybe it wipes the molecular programming. Maybe it's only temporary, but it works for now.
CHEMICAL
27B/6... 27B/6...
All I know for sure is that I need a **hell** of a lot more of it.
27B'6
MGFF-AHHHH!
27B'6
SKRRUKKK-SPPSSHHH!

YYEEEEEHHEHGHG
It spasms and lashes as it dies. Flailing limbs rupture other drums and an acrid stink rises as chemicals intermix in dangerous proportions.
I don't look back.
Dry burn. Ignition. Fireball. Hammerblow.
Thank god the fire drill had gotten the staff out.
FWHOOMF!
Everything burns. Everything they had.
Except perhaps that human imperative to invent for invention's sake. Stern and Spasky followed Dyson. Who'll follow them?
Some damn fool, you can be certain.

We're right back where we started, John.
We still can't be sure if we've won.
HIGHWAY 78, CROSSING THE CHOCOLATE MOUNTAINS...
BLYTHE! BLYTHE!
COME ON! WE HAVE TO HELP DANNY!
BLYTHE DYSON! GET OVER HERE!
RING AROUND THE ROSIE. POCKET FULL OF POSIES. ASHES. ASHES. WE ALL FALL DOWN.
DANNY? COME ON, CHAMP! WAKE UP! WAKE UP!
PLEASE, CHAMP, WAKE UP
MOSSBERG! WHERE ARE YOU? MOSSBERG!
DANNY NEEDS HELP NOW, BADGE!
SKK-RRT-
CHHCHCH-HHH!
Huh?
OH NO!

grnh
Hak! Hak! Hak!
JEEEEEEZUS.
MOSSBERG! PLEASE! PLEASE!
JOHN?
HANG ON, JOHN. HANG ON.
GOTTA CLEAR MY HEAD. FIND STUFF.
YEAH. THAT'S RIGHT. STUFF.
HE-LLO BABY!
THIS IS WHAT I NEED. I THINK.
HOW HARD CAN IT BE?
MOSSBERG! IF YOU'RE GONNA DO SOMETHING . . .
...DO IT QUICK!

I CAN'T RUN FOREVER, YOU HEAR ME?
MOSSBERG! IT'S ALL OVER ME!
ughhnn!
NO!
Oh GEEZ! NO GOOD!
HANG ON, JOHN! JUST HANG ON!
...STUPID TOGGLE SONUVA...
I CAN'T HANG ON!
OKAY THEN...
...DUCK.

KRAKA
THOOOOOMM!
whaddyaknow...
WAY TO GO, BADGE.
10

I run. I hide. I make some calls.
Tarissa finds me after midnight.
SARAH? WHAT H--
JUST DRIVE.
How can I tell her the real truth?
How can I tell her that it'll probably start again? The one thing this has showed me is that it's not the Terminators we should really fear.
It's **mankind** and our terrible ability to survive, an ability we will not lose until we have made sure the machines have **inherited** it.
While I sort out the terrible implications of these new developments, we go to ground.
The next day, we make the mountains.
True to his word, David Mossberg has led our children to safety.
And they've had **adventures** of their own on the way. Our friends the Salcedas have tended Danny Dyson's wounds.
Seems they took out an **800** en route.
I feel **obsolete**.
LET'S TALK.

I tell him about Network and the T-1000.
I explain to him that I think Skynet is now a certainty. No matter how many times we delay its creation, there will always be someone eager to step in and finish what's been started... just to see if they can.
We are our own worst enemy. The nuclear twilight will come.
SO THE FIGHT MAY LAST AWHILE AND IT MIGHT GET DIRTIER.
WE WERE KINDA EXPECTING THAT, WEREN'T WE?
IGGY P
DANNY AND I HAVE BEEN THINKING...
He tells me about the source code. He explains Danny's virus idea and his own long-term plan...
...and for a moment, I'm too surprised to be proud of my son.
John is wise enough, even in a battle of astounding odds, to recognize that a child's imagination can be the children of the future.
"There's no fate but what we make for ourselves", he reminds me with a laugh, Kyle's intensity in his eyes.
NO FATE. WE'RE GOING TO MAKE IT OURSELVES WITH THE LIVES OF THREE BILLION PEOPLE, JOHN. IT SEEMS SO INEVITABLE. THE WAR, JUDGMENT DAY... IT CAN'T BE CHANGED. IT'S OUR FUTURE.
IF IT IS INEVITABLE, MOM, THEN IT ALSO MEANS WE'LL WIN... SOMEDAY.
We'll make it.
One way or another.
END

WHIGHAM

by **Ron Fortier & Alex Ross**

ISBN: 0-7434-7927-0

A FULL-COLOR GRAPHIC NOVEL EVENT!

THE RETURN OF THE FIRST PROFESSIONAL COMICS WORK BY AWARD-WINNING ARTIST ALEX ROSS, AND THE FIRST ORIGINAL GRAPHIC NOVEL EVER BASED ON THE HIT FILM!

Led by an adult John Connor, the resistance movement has battled its way to the gates of Skynet's Colorado stronghold. One problem, though: A new kind of Terminator is waiting for Connor and his soldiers—and she will let nothing stop her from killing the rebel leader. . . .

INTRODUCTION BY JIM KRUEGER

(Earth X, The Clockmaker)

TERMINATOR 2®

THE NEW JOHN CONNOR CHRONICLES

Book 1: DARK FUTURES

by Russell Blackford
ISBN: 0-7434-4511-2

THE FIRST IN A TRILOGY OF ALL-NEW NOVELS BASED ON THE POPULAR FILM!

Following the events of *Terminator 2: Judgment Day,* Sarah Connor and her son, John, had thought they'd been able to alter the future so that neither the artificially intelligent satellite SkyNet nor its Terminator killing machines would ever be created.

But if they were so successful, why, then, are they now being hunted by yet *another* Terminator that's traveled back in time to ensure that John never grows up to be the charismatic leader of the few humans who survived Judgment Day?

And when a band of human warriors from an alternate timeline make an unexpected appearance, have they come to help John—or the cyborg killing machine . . . ?

TERMINATOR 2®

THE NEW JOHN CONNOR CHRONICLES

Book 2: AN EVIL HOUR

by Russell Blackford
ISBN: 0-7434-4511-2

CONTINUING THE TRILOGY OF ALL-NEW NOVELS BASED ON THE POPULAR FILM!

Judgment Day is coming! Following the events of Book 1 (*Dark Futures*), the future war between the human Resistance and the forces of Skynet takes an unusual twist as Terminators from an alternate timeline invade the world of John Connor and his mother, Sarah, seeking to bring about the inevitable war that the Connors had merely delayed with their actions. But another cyborg has traveled across the dimensions to protect John—and nothing is going to prevent her from carrying out her mission!